"You meant to call me?" Mark pointed to his chest. Zoey Coyle, his beautiful, sweet, wonderful trainer, had called him—on purpose?

"Yes." Zoey crossed her arms in front of her chest. "I mean, I shouldn't have. I saw you leave with Myra, and if you have a girlfriend—"

"Myra's not my girlfriend."

"Well, I offered to take you to the store; then I saw you leave with her, and..."

Mark almost fell over from what he was hearing. Was it possible Zoey could be interested in him? *What are you waiting for, Mark?* he chastised himself. "Would you like to go with me today?"

She shook her head. "I didn't mean to make you feel like you have to take me along to the store...."

Mark placed his hand on hers. She looked up at him, and he drank in her chocolate brown eyes. Zoey was too beautiful for words. "I'd really like to go together."

"Okay."

A slight coloring of red made its way up her neck and to her cheeks. She looked even more adorable. The urge to trace her jaw to her lips nearly overwhelmed him. He wanted so much to kiss her.

She cleared her throat. "That doesn't mean I'm going easy on you tonight."

Mark smiled and tapped the end of her nose. "Of course not."

"Get in that pool."

Before he could r

JENNIFER JOHNSON and her unbelievably supportive husband, Albert, are happily married and raising Brooke, Hayley, and Allie, the three cutest young ladies on the planet. Besides being a middle-school teacher, Jennifer loves to read, write, and chauffeur her girls. She is a member of the American Christian Fiction Writers. Blessed beyond measure, Jennifer hopes to always think like a child—bigger than imaginable and with complete faith. Send her a note at jenwrites4god@bellsouth.net.

Books by Jennifer Johnson

HEARTSONG PRESENTS
HP725—By His Hand
HP738—Picket Fence Pursuit
HP766—Pursuing the Goal
HP802—In Pursuit of Peace
HP866—Finding Home
HP882—For Better or Worse

Gaining Love

Jennifer Johnson

Heartsong Presents

This book is dedicated to one of the sweetest women I know, my sister-in-law, Laura Miles. Laura, I am so thankful God placed you in my family. You are a wonderful Christian, wife to my brother, and mother to my precious niece and nephews. You are a treasure!

A note from the Author:
I love to hear from my readers! You may correspond with me by writing:

Jennifer Johnson
Author Relations
PO Box 721
Uhrichsville, OH 44683

ISBN 978-1-60260-847-4

GAINING LOVE

Scripture taken from the HOLY BIBLE, NEW INTERNATIONAL VERSION®. NIV®. Copyright © 1973, 1978, 1984 by International Bible Society. Used by permission of Zondervan. All rights reserved.

All of the characters and events in this book are fictitious. Any resemblance to actual persons, living or dead, or to actual events is purely coincidental.

Our mission is to publish and distribute inspirational products offering exceptional value and biblical encouragement to the masses.

PRINTED IN THE U.S.A.

one

"I'm afraid you're going to have to lose weight."

Mark White cringed at the doctor's words. A decade before, when Mark was a high school football star, those would have been the last words uttered from a physician's lips. He glanced down at his soft center; it had once been firm and strong, sporting a much-coveted six-pack. His buddies often teased him about the excess weight when they got together for Monday night football or Boston Celtics basketball games, but he wasn't the only one who'd put on a few pounds since his late teens and early twenties. In good-natured fun, they all goaded each other now and then.

"Forty pounds would be ideal," continued the dark-haired, physically fit doctor who was probably fifteen years Mark's senior. "And I'm going to give you a prescription. Normally I allow my patients to attempt to alter their diet and exercise first. But your blood pressure is simply too high for me to feel comfortable with that."

Mark swallowed, concern creeping up his spine. When Mark was only a senior in high school, his father died at age forty-two from a stroke. The loss nearly devastated his mother as she cared for Mark's younger sister, who was battling leukemia. Pushing the mountain of memories to the back of his mind, Mark focused on the doctor. The man ripped the prescription off the pad.

"I'm going to start you at a small dose." He scribbled on yet another sheet. "You'll have to take a water pill, which will keep excess fluids away from the heart, but it will also make you urinate often. My suggestion would be to take it in the morning." He ripped that sheet off as well and handed it to Mark. "I want to see you in a month to be sure the medicine is working. Do you have any questions?"

Mark stared at the prescriptions. He hated medicine. His house had been burdened by bottle after bottle his last two years of high school. Blood pressure pills for Dad. Medicines for Maddy's leukemia. Anxiety tablets for Mom. To this day, Mark would hardly ever take a pain reliever for a headache. He normally just tried to squeeze in a quick nap. After all, it wasn't as if his social calendar bulged from abundant activity. Other than Monday night football with the guys and his men's Bible study on Thursday, mainly all Mark did was work, attend church, and spend time with his mom and Maddy.

Mark looked up at the doctor. "No. I don't have any questions."

"Okay then." The doctor extended his hand. "I'll see you in a month."

After accepting the handshake, Mark watched as the doctor walked out. Slipping off the patient bed, Mark looked at himself in the full-length mirror beside the doctor's chair. To see him in his dress slacks and shirt and tie, no one would believe Mark had forty pounds he needed to shed. He was a big guy, six foot five. He was an ex-football player who still sported the broad chest and shoulders as evidence.

But Mark knew he was soft. Too soft. His knees and ankles hurt when he tried to run, especially the left leg, which had been broken his last football season. He felt almost as strong as he'd been in high school, but he also winded easily. At times his heart seemed to beat faster, harder than it should.

At night, when he took off his banker's monkey suit and changed into a comfortable pair of long shorts and a T-shirt, Mark could see the extra weight. And he hated it.

With a sigh, he walked out of the room and to the front desk, where a young blond-haired woman took the sheet from his hand. With barely a glance, she smiled at him then looked at her computer screen. "Dr. Carr wants to see you back in a month."

Mark studied the receptionist as she scanned the available appointments. Not too many years ago, the woman probably would have giggled and flirted with him, and Mark would have sucked in the attention. *That was before I accepted Christ into my heart.*

And before I gained all this extra weight.

Mark inwardly chastised himself for such superficial thoughts, and yet the physical concern was not to be taken lightly. His father had packed on an extra hundred pounds in the last few years before he died. The doctor had warned him repeatedly that his blood pressure was out of control. Mark didn't want to die young as his father had. God had a plan for Mark's life, even if it never involved anything more than working at the bank and caring for his mom and sister. He wouldn't devastate them the way his father had.

"How about this day and time?" The receptionist handed him a reminder card.

"That will be fine." He took the card and turned to the door. Making his way to his car, he spied a fitness place. *First step: Join a gym.*

Mark drove to one of Wilmington's largest fitness facilities. *It shouldn't be too busy. Not yet anyway. With Thanksgiving in a few weeks and Christmas over a month away, people won't want to think about their waistlines until New Year's.* Walking inside, he couldn't help but notice that most of the people who appeared to be around his age—in their mid- to late twenties—seemed physically fit. The flabby ones were a decade or more older than him.

Out of the corner of his eye, Mark saw an obese man trying to bench press a weight that Mark would have snubbed his nose at when he was a teen.

"You can do it." A gorgeous redhead stood beside the man, encouraging him. "Come on. Just a little farther."

Mark watched the man's face redden as he held his breath, trying to get the weight to the bar. The woman lifted her hand over the bar, ready to help him if he couldn't push it all the way up.

She doesn't look strong enough to lift that weight, especially if the guy can't do it.

The crimson color of the guy's skin deepened until Mark feared a vein would burst in his head. The bar started to tilt, and before Mark could process what was happening, the tiny redhead lifted the bar up and set it in its place. The man sat up, straining for breath.

"You got five reps in." The pretty trainer patted his back. "You did good."

Mark looked at the bar. The guy couldn't have been benching more than 100 or 120 pounds, and he was a young guy. Probably younger than Mark. *The extra weight must make him soft.*

The thought of some young cutie having to lift a bar off him flashed through his mind, slamming his ego. God had changed Mark over the years, and he'd grown in leaps and bounds in the humility department. He glanced at the red-haired woman who couldn't weigh more than his left leg. If she had to spot him—actually lift a weight off him—well, a man had his pride.

Mark turned toward the door. He couldn't join this gym. He'd have to work out at home. Start running. Buy a bench. Check out exercises on the Internet. He'd talk to his buddies, Bruce and Chris. They might have a good idea of where he should start.

"May I help you, sir?"

Mark pivoted toward the voice behind him. The man, though probably a little older than Mark, appeared to be in terrific shape.

"Are you interested in joining our facility?" The man gestured around the expansive room.

"I was thinking about it, but I may just try going at it on my own." Mark started to turn back toward the door.

"At least let me give you a tour. Show you what we offer."

Mark turned back around and scanned what he could see of the place. A vision of telling his mom he would be taking blood pressure medicine shot through his mind. He looked back at the guy. "Okay. What do you offer?"

❧

Zoey Coyle set her shoulder bag on the table then dropped into the chair. Overwhelmingly whipped, she'd already led two personal training sessions and a water aerobics class. She looked at her watch. It was only noon. "Only five more hours," she grumbled as she pulled a turkey and lettuce sandwich on wheat bread and an apple from her bag.

One of the three credit card bills she'd received in the mail that morning stuck to the sandwich baggie. After pulling it off, she reached into the oversized purse and grabbed the other two. Putting the envelopes to the right of her lunch, she focused on retrieving her sandwich. She arranged the lettuce until it fit just right between the slices of bread then took a bite.

The sandwich had little taste already, but when her gaze kept wandering to the bills at her right, Zoey found it difficult to swallow. She rolled her eyes and scooped the bills into her hand. *Just get it over with. Stewing over it won't change how much you owe.*

Sliding her fingernail beneath the envelope's flap, she noted her acrylic nails were almost in need of a fill-in. Actually, with Christmas coming, she'd want to get red tips in celebration of the season. *I can't think of that right now. How much did I put on these cards this month?* Zoey tried to pinpoint in her mind her various shopping excursions. She hoped the totals wouldn't be as bad as the nudging feeling she had deep down in her chest.

She opened the first. The bill was higher than she'd expected, and it should have been the smallest one. Her heart fell. Before she could talk herself out of it, she opened the second and third. Staring at the totals, she reached for her sandwich and took a big bite. "Over a thousand," she mumbled.

Shaking her head, she shoved the envelopes back into the bottom of the bag. How had she gotten herself into so much credit card debt? She thought of the trip she'd made to the mall to buy a new pair of tennis shoes, but she couldn't resist the sale and bought a couple of pairs of casual shoes as well. Her mind then drifted to the trip she'd made to buy a winter coat, when she'd also bought a dress that caught her eye. She couldn't even remember all the cute outfits she'd bought for her precious Micah. And if Zoey bought something for Micah, she had to buy a little something for Ellie, too. Then she'd usually end up getting a gift for her little twin sisters.

She scooped up her bottle of water and took a long drink. There was no sense in reliving every shopping trip she'd made. It was time for action. She smacked the bottle down on the table. *If I work an extra day per week for the next two months, and only take five days off at Christmas break to visit Micah. . .*

The thought nearly ripped Zoey's heart in two. Since she'd started college, she'd spent every break staying with her mom, Harold, and her younger sisters. And she enjoyed seeing them, but it was Micah, her precious three-year-old, she treasured visiting the most.

At seventeen, Zoey had been rebellious toward God and her mother. Eventually she'd ended up pregnant. God used that time to woo her back to Himself, but Zoey still faced consequences. One of them was she knew she couldn't care properly for her unborn child. She allowed her uncle Cam and his wife, Sadie, to adopt him.

The moment she handed her son to Sadie washed over her anew. It felt like she'd pried off a vital part of her body and given it willingly to someone else to nurture and love. She had to trust someone else with a piece of herself. She'd never felt such a connection with another human being as she'd felt with Micah. And yet she'd handed him over to her aunt Sadie. It had been the hardest choice she'd ever made.

Only five days. The mounting credit card debt was proof enough that Zoey wasn't ready to care for anyone in addition to herself. Because of her lack of restraint, she'd have to work extra hours to get rid of the balances before she graduated from college in May.

I need to learn to do better with my money, because my paycheck as a dietician won't be very much higher than it is now. The monthly inner scolding hadn't seemed to help her refrain from using her credit cards. Aside from cutting them up, the thought of which sent her heart fluttering and made her hands clammy, Zoey didn't know what to do to make herself stop completely.

"Zoey, how much longer is your lunch?"

Zoey startled at the voice of her manager behind her. She turned toward the man who was double her age but looked like he'd just stepped out of a bodybuilder magazine. "Uh, what time is it?" She glanced from him to her watch. "Wow!" She took a big bite of her sandwich. "Only ten minutes," she mumbled through her full mouth.

"Okay, good. I have a new client for you."

Zoey nodded. " 'Kay." She took an oversized bite of her

apple. Having a new client would help her pay down some of her debt. *I know what I'll do to stop spending. I'll put my cards in my dresser. That way they're still available for an emergency, but I won't be able to use them when I run over to the Concord Mall.*

She took a long swig of her water, practically shoving her food down her throat. She took two more bites of her sandwich and another gulp of water.

Or maybe I could stick them in a bowl of water and freeze them. Didn't I see that on a movie one time? She stood and slipped her bag onto her shoulder. After throwing away her trash, she took another bite of apple then pitched it as well.

Of course, I'll still need to make myself stay away from Internet shopping. My credit card number just pops up right before my eyes for a few of my favorite places. Zoey growled as she walked into the employee locker room and put away her bag. Making her way back to the main fitness area two minutes before her lunchtime officially ended, Zoey scanned the room for her manager.

She found Zeke, noting the supertall man beside him—a good five inches over six feet. She couldn't see the guy's face yet, but his height alone suggested he had to be at least two times Zoey's weight. *Spotting him on a bench press should be a lot of fun, if not impossible.* Zoey smiled at the thought, but she did enjoy a challenge.

two

"Hi. I'm Zoey Coyle." The adorable redhead Mark had watched earlier stood before him with her hand extended. Before Mark had a chance to move, she looked at Zeke. "I'm assuming he's my new client."

Oh no. Mark closed his eyes. *A pretty, tiny woman?* What was this manager, Zeke, thinking? Mark was gargantuan compared to her. He opened his eyes. Her wrist bone looked about as thick as his pinky finger. Mark realized she still waited for his handshake, so he grabbed her hand gently in his. Her grip was firm for a gal who couldn't weigh an ounce over a hundred, but still. . .

"Zoey, this is Mark White."

Zeke patted his back as he spoke to the small woman, who, now that Mark looked at her more closely, appeared to be younger than Mark's little sister. *How many years could she possibly be out of high school?*

"It's a pleasure to meet you, Mr. White." His trainer widened her stance and placed her hands on her hips in a way that suggested authority. "Did Zeke explain what we'll do first?"

Okay, so the gal wasn't in high school. Much too authoritative for that, but she couldn't be too many years over twenty. Mark cleared his throat. "You'd like to ask me a few questions first."

"That's right." The woman nodded to her manager. "Thanks for introducing us, Zeke. I'll take it from here."

Mark watched as Zeke walked away, realizing he'd forgotten his trainer's name. So stunned by her dainty appearance, he hadn't paid close enough attention. *The fact that she has large, dark chocolate eyes and the creamiest skin I've ever seen—not to mention her thick, full lips and face shaped almost like a heart—that has nothing to do with it.*

Mark shook his head. What was he thinking? Forty pounds of excess weight. That was what he needed to focus on.

"If you'll follow me, I'll get the paperwork we need and we'll head to the conference room."

Without a response, Mark followed her past the front desk and into a small room with a table and chairs. Various athletic and physical fitness posters adorned the walls. He also noted a scale in the far corner.

She's going to weigh me. The realization humbled him. Maybe he wouldn't have cared so much if he hadn't been in such good shape when he was younger or if she weren't so attractive. Since when did a man care about what he weighed? *But I do.*

"Go ahead and have a seat." She pointed toward a chair and she sat in one across from it. "Okay, your name is Mark White. If you don't mind, I'd like to call you Mark, and of course, you may call me Zoey."

"That's fine." Mark rolled her name around in his mind. He had never met a Zoey, except his aunt's dog, but he wasn't sure the trainer would be happy to know that.

"Your age?"

"I'm twenty-seven."

Zoey scribbled on the paper. "Yeah? When's your birthday?"

"April twenty-first."

"Well, how cool is that. I'll be twenty-two on the twenty-seventh." She chewed the tip of her pen, her gaze focusing upward. Taking the pen from her mouth, she grinned. "You're exactly six years and six days older than me. Cool."

Mark lifted his eyebrows. The innocent expression on her face, as well as her bubbly and straightforward disposition, intrigued him. "That is interesting."

She looked back at the paper. "We'll get your weight after I finish asking all the other questions."

Mark squirmed. He didn't want her to get his weight. He would have preferred to keep track of it on his own, but he knew that would defeat the purpose of having a trainer. According to Zeke, Zoey was the best he had. Mark hoped so. He didn't want to be on high blood pressure medication for the rest of his life. When he got his weight down and his diet controlled, he planned to see if Dr. Carr would take him off the prescription.

"So what do you do for a living? Does your job keep you active?"

"I'm a bank loan officer, so no. I pretty much crunch numbers all day."

Zoey huffed. "Me, too, but not for my job. For my spending habits." She swatted the air with her hand. A nervous smile tilted her lips. "Sorry. I don't usually make so many silly comments. I mean, I'm not *bad* with money; I just need a little more discipline." She shook her head. "I have no idea why I just said—let's just go on to the next question."

Mark smiled. Zoey was as nervous as he was. He wondered if she felt uncomfortable with asking so many personal questions or if she could tell he was attracted to her. *Could that even be possible? A gorgeous woman like her—*

No way. That wasn't a possibility, so he might as well get the idea out of his head right now. Trying to relax, he folded his hands together on top of the table. "I could always help you with that if you wanted."

"It's just I graduate from college in May and I don't want any debt."

"What are you majoring in?"

"Dietetics."

Mark leaned back in the chair. "I'd say you and I could help each other quite a bit. Not only do I need a trainer; I need a better diet."

Zoey cocked her head, studying him. "Have you recently been diagnosed with a medical condition?"

Mark nodded. "High blood pressure." He patted his pants pocket. "I have two prescriptions to fill."

"Your doctor didn't want to try diet and exercise first?"

"Nope. It's too high."

Concern etched her brow. "But you're so young."

Mark exhaled a long breath. "I know. My dad died from a stroke when he was only forty-two. He battled high blood pressure and obesity. I don't want to follow in his footsteps."

"I'd say not." Zoey stood to her feet. "Stand up."

Taken aback, Mark did as she asked, and Zoey felt his wrists and arms, a determined look on her face. It warmed Mark that she would care so quickly for the medical well-being of one of her clients. He wanted to think she found him attractive but pushed the ridiculous notion aside. She probably had young, hulky men swarming her all the time.

"You're definitely a big-boned man." She kept hold of his hand as she walked to the scale. "Let's see what you weigh."

He stepped onto the scale, cringing at the high number he saw. Forcing himself to smile, he patted his belly. "Definitely a big boy."

Without a word, she turned him around to measure his height. She scribbled on her pad again then placed it on the table. Touching his bicep, she smiled. "We can do this. Six foot five. Two hundred eighty pounds. If you do as I say, we'll shed those extra forty to fifty pounds in four months or less."

Mark warmed at her soft touch. Whatever she said, he'd do it.

What am I doing? Zoey quickly removed her hand from the

man's arm. Something about Mark drew her. Sure, he was handsome enough with his dark blond hair and deep brown eyes. So deep brown that Zoey found herself wanting to study them to guess the thoughts behind those pools. And his scent—whatever cologne the man wore attracted her like a strawberry to angel food cake.

But his weight, his sheer size—Zoey was normally drawn to men closer to her height and on the smaller side. And yet she was attracted to this hulk of a man. Really attracted.

"Let's talk a bit more." She motioned for him to sit in the chair again. "Have you had any injuries that would keep you from using specific exercise equipment?"

"I broke my left leg my senior year in high school. It bothers me at times when I run." She noticed a blush creeping up his neck. "It may just be because of the extra weight."

Zoey wrote down the information then finished her questions. She knew many fitness centers simply allowed their clients to fill out the form and then give it to the trainer to skim before the session. Zoey loved that Zeke required the face-to-face interviews. She almost always got a feel for the route she'd want to take with her clients.

"Can you swim?"

"Yes."

She studied Mark. "How well?"

"I was a lifeguard during the summers when I was a teenager."

"Perfect." She picked up the stack of papers. "We're going to start with swimming laps." She shuffled his information to the front page. "It looks like Zeke has set you up for Mondays and Wednesdays at 5:30 and Fridays at 6:30." She looked at Mark. "Tomorrow is Friday. Are you starting tomorrow or Monday?"

"Tomorrow."

A smile bowed her lips, and Zoey found herself looking

forward to seeing Mark the following day. "Don't forget your swimsuit."

Mark grimaced, and Zoey laughed louder than she intended. "Don't worry. It will be fun."

Mark studied her for several moments, and Zoey felt heat rushing up her cheeks. She wished she could read the thoughts behind those mysterious dark eyes. A slow smile spread his lips as his eyes shifted to contain a glimmer of mischief. "Yes, I think it will be."

When Mark walked out the door, Zoey placed her hands on her cheeks. She could feel the warmth. Racing to the far wall, she peeked into the small mirror that hung there. Yep, her white, almost translucent complexion sported a nice beet shade. *Why did I have to get so embarrassed?*

Sighing, she glanced down at her watch. She was teaching water aerobics in twenty minutes. Barely enough time to get to her locker, change into her suit, and head to the pool area. She placed Mark's papers into the file Zeke had given her. *I'll take these home. Go over my notes. I'll look up some good recipes for people with high blood pressure.*

Zoey's excitement swelled as she walked into the locker room. She loved helping people come up with healthy menus for their specific medical needs. She couldn't wait to finish school and hopefully get a job in a hospital or possibly a nursing home.

Opening her locker, Zoey spied a new text message on her cell phone. *It's from Brittany.* Her heart raced as she thought of her younger sister and the choices she'd been making lately. She opened the text. "Out with Neil. Don't wait up," she muttered.

Zoey's heart plunged as she pushed a response as quickly as her fingers would move. "Think, Brit. Think. Go home."

She shoved her phone into her bag and scooped out her

swimsuit. *God, what can I do or say to get Brit to think clearly?*

Zoey recalled an incident only one week before when her sister was crying on her shoulder because of the ugly things her boyfriend had said in front of their friends. Zoey had witnessed his inappropriate comments toward other women right in front of Brittany. Zoey simply didn't understand why her sister would allow someone to treat her that way.

Zoey thought of the boy she'd been head over heels in love with during her senior year of high school. Dark-haired, mysterious, older—she had thought he was the most wonderful person in the world. No one could convince her otherwise.

God, I don't want Brittany to go through what I've gone through. I don't want her to make the same mistakes as me.

"Can a mother forget the baby at her breast and have no compassion on the child she has borne? Though she may forget, I will not forget you! See, I have engraved you on the palms of my hands. . . ." As the scripture from Isaiah sifted through her mind, she could feel the Spirit's nudging to remember that Brittany's name was engraved on His palms as well.

Zoey grabbed a towel from the locker room closet and made her way to the pool. She would trust God and encourage and love her sister every chance she could. And for now she'd focus on the women in her water aerobics class.

three

Mark glanced down at his watch. *One thirty,* he inwardly growled. He was thirty minutes over his lunch break. Betty, the bank's manager, knew that Mark had a doctor visit and might be late, but he never intended to be a full half hour late. There was no telling what his colleague Kevin Fink would say. The man seemed to find pleasure in goading Mark every opportunity he had. *I can hear Kevin now.* He pushed open the front door of the bank.

"Did your watch malfunction, White?"

Mark turned toward Kevin's voice. His coworker leaned against the door frame of his office. *Just as I expected. The guy always has something to say.*

"Were you waiting for me, Kevin?" Mark could hear the irritation in his voice. He forced himself to smile at Kevin. No matter what it was, be it clients, paperwork, even ties and haircuts, Kevin liked to annoy him. Occasionally the younger man would mutter about Mark's faith. It was those comments that Mark believed were the source of the animosity. Kevin had a problem with him because he was a Christian. Mark tried to show God's love to the guy.

Most days.

"Must be nice to come strolling in to work whenever you want." Kevin chuckled and winked at the teller they'd hired a month ago.

Mark knew the man tried to sound as if he was teasing, but Mark knew better. Too many times Kevin had gone behind Mark's back to make it look as if he could do a better job.

Which is why I'm glad two of my stronger qualities are organization and documentation.

Before Mark could respond, Betty Grimes approached him and put her hand on his arm. "How'd your appointment go, Mark?"

"Blood pressure's a little high." He patted his belly. "Gotta lose some weight."

The gray-haired woman peered up at him through thick, small-framed glasses. "You don't want to mess with that, Mark. Do what the doctor says. You're too young to end up on medication."

Mark nodded, deciding not to tell the woman who treated him like a nephew that he had already been given two prescriptions.

"You know what?" Kevin snapped his fingers, the tone of his voice too syrupy. "We should have a 'biggest loser' contest at the bank."

Betty patted Kevin on the back. "That's a terrific idea."

Kevin beamed, and Mark wanted to barf. The man would do anything to gain the boss's favor. *If he'd focus more on doing his job and less on how to avoid it, she might. . .*

"I've been wanting to lose some weight for years," Betty continued.

"Oh no." Kevin shook his head. "You don't need to lose any weight, Betty. You look great."

Mark looked from Kevin to the short bank manager. Betty needed to shed several pounds, and the truth was she'd put on more weight in the years that Mark had worked there. Betty knew it. Mark knew it. Kevin knew it. Mark would never consider being cruel about a person's weight, but he wouldn't lie, either. He studied Betty. "I know I'll physically feel better if I shed a few pounds."

Betty's eyes glimmered. "Me, too." She tapped her lips

with her index finger, a sign she was mulling her thoughts around in her mind. "I'll get some sign-ups together, write up some goals and rules. Maybe even come up with a prize." She turned back toward her office. "This was a great idea."

"Glad I thought of it," Kevin yelled toward her. He looked at Mark, a scowl contorting his face. "Think I'll sign up, too."

Mark frowned as he sized up his much shorter colleague. The man couldn't have weighed much over 160. "You really don't need to lose any weight."

"A little weight loss never hurt anyone."

❧

Zoey dropped the bags of groceries onto the countertop. She glanced at the clock while pulling a container of sliced turkey and a fresh tomato from a bag. *It's barely past five. I'd hoped I would catch Brittany before she left.*

A sinking feeling weighed Zoey's gut. Neil was not a guy her sister needed to be hanging out with. He was all brawn and little brains. And absolutely no faith. Zoey remembered the time he'd grabbed her sister's arm a little too tightly when they'd been having an argument. Though Brittany swore Neil had never hurt her, Zoey feared one day he might.

Saying a silent prayer on her sister's behalf, Zoey walked to the slow cooker and lifted the lid. The aroma of roast beef and vegetables encouraged a growl from her stomach. She poked the tender meat with a fork. "Just the way I like it."

As she grabbed a plate out of the cabinet, the doorbell rang. "Who could that be?"

She walked to the front door and peeked through the peephole. A smile formed on her lips as she opened the door. "Harold? What are you doing here?"

Her stepfather wrapped her in a hug that nearly stole her breath away. "I had a job in Wilmington today, and since I haven't seen my oldest girls in a while, I thought I'd stop by for a visit." He released her and sucked in a deep breath. "Mmm. Smells like I'm just in time."

"In a while? We just saw you last week. Remember, I had last Saturday off, and—"

Harold shrugged. "That's a while to me."

Zoey laughed as she motioned him inside. "You always seem to pick the right time. It's almost as if a bird tells you—"

He straightened his shoulders and rubbed his belly. "Not a bird. A man just knows when there's good food to be eaten."

"That's funny. 'Cause I talked to Mom today and told her I had a roast in the Crock-Pot."

"What a coincidence. I talked to your mom today, too, and she told me you had a roast in the Crock-Pot."

Zoey laughed. "Head on into the kitchen. You know where the plates are."

She followed Harold into the kitchen. They fixed their plates then sat at the small table in the living/dining room. Her stepfather prayed over their food then stabbed his fork into a potato. "So where's Brittany?"

"Out with Neil."

Harold stopped chewing and let out a sigh. The wrinkles on his forehead smoothed as he contemplated Zoey's response.

Thankfulness filled Zoey's heart for the man who cared so much about her and her sisters. Four years ago she felt only animosity and anger toward the man who seemed to try to steal her daddy's place only a few years after his death. But Harold's character, patience, and love for the Lord, her mother, and them had shone through until Zoey couldn't help but fall in love with the man as a second father.

Zoey rolled her fork between her fingers. "I've been praying for her, trying to talk sense into her."

"We've been praying, too." Harold stabbed a piece of meat.

"Wish I could pop some sense into her, but she's a young adult. She knows God. She knows what is right."

Zoey couldn't help but grin as she thought of her and Harold's first meetings. "I know you wanted to pop some sense into me."

Harold raised one eyebrow. "The first time I saw you?"

Zoey nodded.

"No. The first time I saw you, I wanted to wash the black out of your hair and scrub it off your face."

Zoey smiled, though a twinge of pain mingled with guilt swept over her at the memory of her last two years of high school. She'd rebelled against God and her mother after her father's death, delving into dark thoughts, dark hair, dark makeup, dark clothes, dark friends. . . *Thank You, God, for pulling me out of that.*

The quick praise made her think of Micah, the consequence of her sinful actions. Pregnancy her senior year of high school hadn't been easy. Giving her baby to her uncle and aunt to raise had been excruciating. And yet God had used what she believed to be a punishment, a consequence, as an indescribable blessing. Cam and Sadie received a son they never would have been able to have on their own biologically; Zoey received a reestablished relationship with her heavenly Father and the opportunity to be a part of her son's life.

Zoey wiped her mouth with a napkin. "So how are Micah and the girls?"

"Micah is great. Nice, quiet little man who adores Cam and does everything his daddy asks him to do. The twins. . ." Harold pointed to his fully grayed hair. "Well, do you see the top of my head? They've put the gray up there."

"I thought I did that."

"You got it going. Rebecca and Rachel finished it out."

Zoey giggled, picturing her adorable half sisters.

"I'm not kidding. Do you know what those two little rascals did the other day? They figured out that if one of them holds the lock to the back door gate and the other one pushes, then they can escape the backyard." Harold rubbed his temples. "Your poor mother was trying to do the dishes when she looked out the kitchen window and spied the girls trying to get into the car. She nearly had a heart attack."

"They are—active. That's for sure."

"Active?" Harold shook his head. "The preschool teachers are already making their rooms Smith-twins-proof."

Zoey leaned back in her chair and laughed, knowing that Harold's comment was completely true. "I can't wait to get home to see everyone."

"Christmas break's in less than a month, right?"

Zoey nodded. She didn't have the heart to admit she wouldn't be able to stay the full time.

"So how is school going?"

"Good."

"Any new guys in your life?"

A vision of Mark slipped into her mind. She didn't know why. The guy was nothing like the kind of men to whom she was normally attracted. *Do I even know who I'm attracted to? I went for the dark, older guys in high school, and I've gone out with a few men in college, some muscular, but most small and thin. Who am I attracted to?* As soon as the question popped into her mind, she thought of the many conversations she'd had with God about His will for her life. The man she wanted to be attracted to was whatever man God had for her.

She glanced over at Harold. "No. No guys for me. I'm still waiting on God's guidance on that."

Harold patted her hand. "Good girl." He stood, scooped up his plate and hers, and headed toward the kitchen.

"I can do the dishes, Harold."

He scowled at her. "Do you really think I'd just show up for dinner without at least helping out with the dishes?"

"No. You wouldn't." Zoey joined him. He handed her clean dishes from the dishwasher and she put them away.

Harold rinsed off a dirty dish and stuck it in the top tray. "Try to bring Brittany with you when you come home, okay?"

"I will."

❧

Mark struggled into the way-too-small khaki pants. Minutes before, he'd pulled the pair off a hanger in the closet without considering that he hadn't worn them in a few months. *I've already ironed them. I'm going to wear them.* He sucked in a deep breath and fastened the button. "Got it."

He allowed a slow exhale as he adjusted the knot of his tie. "They're a little tight." He dug his index finger beneath the waist of the pants, flattening the white undershirt and the button-down dress shirt. Peering in the mirror above his dresser, he smiled. "But I got them on."

Opening his dresser drawer, he pulled out a pair of black socks, sat on the edge of the bed, then lifted his right foot to his left knee. Before he could get the sock over his foot, the button popped off his waistband and hit the mirror with a loud *smack.*

"That's just great." Mark stood and pulled off the pants. After wadding them up and tossing them on the floor, he grabbed another pair out of the closet. With exaggerated effort, he yanked out the ironing board and popped it open. He turned on the iron then turned and stared into the mirror. He snarled at his reflection.

Men weren't supposed to care this much about their physique. Many sitcoms paraded overweight men, making them known for their laziness, lack of common sense, or both. Those men seemed to welcome their obesity, allowing it to be the punch line of many of the jokes. "But I don't want to be a joke."

Mark stared at his too-thick waist and spongy thighs. He touched his biceps, noting their softness beneath the sleeve. "Once upon a time, I was strong. Rock solid."

His mind wandered to some of the reality shows he'd seen advertised. A lot of the men, many older than his twenty-seven years, were in supreme condition. They looked good, felt good, probably got good reports from their doctors.

Mark cringed at the thought. He'd talked with his mom on the phone last night, but he didn't tell her about the high blood pressure. Since his father's death she'd been taking medicine for anxiety and depression, and he didn't want to upset her or his sister. It was his job to protect them, not cause them to worry.

The light on the iron started to flash, notifying him it was hot enough. He picked it up and began pressing the pants a size bigger than the khaki pair he'd thrown on the floor. Tonight he would start training with Zoey.

He frowned when he thought of the adorable redhead who would witness his struggle to get back in shape. Part of him wanted to call the gym and cancel. Remembering his inability to resist temptation at the fast-food restaurant last night, he shook the desire away. Yes, he would probably humiliate himself in front of the beautiful woman, but he didn't have a choice. He needed help.

four

"I need help." Zoey stared at the bag that held the new skirt and shirt she'd bought from her favorite department store.

Her trip to the Concord Mall had started in innocence. She simply needed to get a new set of acrylic nails. She'd gone to the bank, withdrawn only the amount needed for the nail technician, then parked right in front of the shop. *The only problem is the nail place is right beside my favorite department store, and they were having such a good winter sale.* She pulled the new clothes out of the bag. *And I didn't have a new outfit for Christmas, and these were on sale for 25 percent off. Then with the additional 20 percent off for using my department store credit card. . .*

She flopped onto the couch, allowing the new clothes to fall onto the coffee table. "I promised myself I wouldn't put another penny on my credit cards." She picked up the new pair of dangling earrings. "At least I bought these with cash," she said in an attempt to comfort herself.

It didn't work.

Frustrated, she stood up and walked into the bathroom. She turned on the shower. A headache had wended its way up her neck and into the back of her head. Stress, no doubt.

She stepped into the shower, allowing the hot stream to soothe the stress in her neck and back. She was a mood shopper, a stress shopper, a binge shopper. Whatever it was called, Zoey knew she shopped for the way it made her feel, not because she needed the items.

"God, this isn't good. I'm not glorifying You when I spend

money I don't have. Forgive me, Lord. Show me how to use restraint."

Zoey turned off the water, wrapped a towel around her, then stepped out of the tub. "Before I head to the gym, I'll have to make a quick stop at the mall to take back the outfit."

❧

Zoey stared at the large red-and-white SALE signs plastered on the windows of her favorite store in the mall. She watched as an ultra-thin, thirtyish woman walked out the glass door. Her outfit, a name-brand red-and-white getup that Zoey had drooled over many times before, was impeccable. The woman's long blond hair was cut in perfect choppy layers well past her shoulders. And that purse! Zoey bit her bottom lip. *I practically had to throw myself out of the store to keep myself from buying that purse earlier today.*

She glanced down at the bag containing her new Christmas outfit. Pulling out the green-and-white-patterned blouse, she caressed the silky material. The purse would have matched perfectly with Zoey's outfit. *But if I had to charge to get this outfit, then I don't need it.*

She imagined walking into the store and placing the newly purchased clothes on the counter. What would she tell the clerk when she asked why Zoey was returning the merchandise? Zoey gazed into her rearview mirror. "I have to return these items because I put them on my credit card, and I have a problem with spending too much on my credit card, and so my conscience is telling me I have to bring these back."

She growled as she flipped the mirror away from her reflection. Her heartbeat quickened as she envisioned shoppers waiting impatiently behind her as the clerk scanned the clothes. *What if she has to call a manager?*

Zoey shook her head. She hated to be the center of attention, a 180-degree turnaround from the way she had been in high school. Wearing a dark ensemble every day, she had thrived on the attention, negative or positive, she received from her clothes and actions. Since Micah's birth, so much had shifted in Zoey's mind, heart, and soul. Now, the only group attention she could handle was when she led an aerobic class of some sort. She exhaled a long breath as she tucked the blouse back in the bag. "I can't do it."

She shoved the key in the ignition then turned on the car. She pulled out of the parking space, heading toward the road. "It was only $55. I really like the outfit." She tapped the steering wheel. "I'll just have to pay it off. Lord, help me not to spend any more."

⁂

Mark had avoided the workroom all day. Betty told him she'd put a sign-up sheet for their "biggest loser" contest on the counter. He wondered at the timing, believing most employees wouldn't be interested in joining a weight competition before the holidays. To his thinking, January seemed to be a better time. Nevertheless, several times throughout the day Betty had slipped into his office to let him know who'd signed up so far. She had talked with the night custodian about the contest, and even he'd stopped by a few hours ago to sign up. It was a good thing. Too many of the people he worked with were overweight. They needed to encourage each other to live a healthier lifestyle. Still, it bothered him to admit his weight gain.

He looked up at the clock. He had to be at the gym in less than an hour. *I might as well get in there and sign up.*

Mark pushed open the door and spied Kevin signing the sheet Betty had left out. Mark frowned. "What are you doing, Kevin?"

He turned around and scowled at Mark. "Signing up for the competition. Just like I said yesterday."

"But I thought you were kidding."

"Why would I be kidding?"

"Because you're thin. You don't need to lose any weight."

Kevin moved closer to Mark. He straightened his shoulders, peering up at Mark. "You just don't want me to sign up because you know I'll beat you."

Mark blew out a breath. His colleague was wacko. The competition he felt with Mark was absurd. It made no sense. Their jobs were equal as far as position and pay, and to Mark's knowledge, no one higher up was planning to retire, allowing one of them to move up. "You're challenging the wrong guy, Kev."

Kevin poked Mark's belly and smiled. "Really?"

Fury raced through Mark's veins. He had no idea what his colleague's problem was, but he'd just about had all he could take. If a guy had poked him like that a decade before, Mark would have punched him in the face. He grabbed the pen from Kevin's hand then walked to the sign-up sheet and quickly scrawled his signature. "I guess we'll have to wait and see what happens, little man."

Kevin huffed. "Real Christian-like," he mumbled as he walked out of the workroom.

Mark pounded the side of his fist on the countertop. Once again, he'd allowed his colleague to get under his skin. And once again, Kevin was right. Mark acted anything but Christlike. Mark knew Christ didn't want him to be a doormat, but he also knew that Kevin routinely tried to goad him; therefore, the correct response would have been simply to turn the other cheek. Mark growled as he walked out of the workroom and toward his office. *Forgive me yet again, Lord. You've worked on my pride more than anything else over the years. Obviously, I still have some growing to do.*

He grabbed his things, locked his office, and headed out

the door. All the way to his car and all the way to the gym, Mark prayed that God would help him be a better witness to his colleague. Once at the gym, he picked up his gym bag and jumped out of the car. "Help me focus on losing weight for the right reasons, and not just to beat Kevin."

He pushed open the door and inhaled the mixture of sweat, metal, and rubber. Despite the embarrassment he felt that a beautiful, young, tiny woman would be his trainer, he looked forward to this workout. He was ready to feel better.

A familiar figure caught his eye. He turned to the right and saw Kevin walking on a treadmill. His heart seemed to plunge into his gut. *Isn't it bad enough that Zoey has to train me? Now I have to share a gym with Kevin.*

The smart-aleck comments he'd have to endure sped through his mind. The last thing he wanted to do was train anywhere near Kevin Fink. The urge to turn around nearly swallowed him whole. It seemed whenever he walked into this gym, he wanted nothing more than to walk back out.

"Hey, Mark."

He turned at the sound of Zoey's voice. Her hair was pulled up in two knots at the top of her head. The style made her look younger and even more adorable. "Hi, Zoey."

"You ready to get started?"

"Sure."

"Okay. Head to the lockers and get changed. Meet me at the pool."

Mark nodded. He glanced at Kevin as he walked toward the locker room. The guy had already left his treadmill and was walking toward the pool. "That doesn't surprise me," Mark mumbled to himself. "It's going to be a long hour."

After changing into his swimming trunks, Mark walked into the pool area. Zoey was already in the water. After a quick glance around, he was surprised he didn't see Kevin anywhere.

"Okay, Mark. Go ahead and get in the water."

Surprised at the excitement he felt at swimming a few laps, Mark jumped in the water beside Zoey. The cold rush stole his breath, but within moments his body adjusted and the water felt pleasant and refreshing.

Zoey led him through a few warm-up water exercises that he'd never seen before. He wondered if they'd actually do any good, but he'd chosen to pay to have a trainer, so he'd do what she said.

She ducked her head under the water then smoothed her hair away from her face. Her clear complexion glistened in the water, and Mark found himself wanting to touch her skin with the back of his hand.

"You ready to start swimming laps?"

He nodded and smiled as she grabbed the side of the pool. "Are you going to swim with me?"

"Sure." She frowned. "We're in this together. I'll encourage you every step, or lap, of the way."

Mark had to admit he liked the sound of that, and there was something about the way she said it that seemed personal, as if she wanted to get to know him. *Forget it, White. You're in dreamland. The knockout redhead is not interested in you.* "Okay. So how many laps are we doing?"

She bit her bottom lip, an adorable puzzled expression on her face. "I'm really not sure. I'd like to start swimming some so that I can get a feel for how much you should do to start out."

"Okay. Let's go."

Mark pushed off the side of the pool. They swam one lap, then another, then another. Soon his legs and arms burned at the exercise. But it felt good. Better than he expected, and he found himself enjoying each stroke.

Finally finished, Zoey hopped out of the pool and sat on the side. "That was terrific, Mark. You're in better shape than

I thought. We're going to get that blood pressure down in no time."

Mark jumped out and sat beside her. "You know what, that did feel great. I should have joined years ago." He shook his head. "I don't know why I didn't."

"Well, you're here now." Zoey stood and wrung out her hair in the pool. "Let's get changed and head for the weights."

"All right." Mark walked into the locker room. Already he felt stronger and healthier. *Thank You, God. This is a good thing.*

❧

Zoey patted Mark's shoulder. "You did great. The first session is over."

She watched as he wiped perspiration from his face with a towel. He blew out a long breath then looked up at her from the weight bench. Zoey's stomach flipped when his deep brown eyes peered into hers. "It felt great, too."

He stood to his full height and Zoey found herself craning her neck to look him in the eye. "You'll probably be pretty sore tomorrow, but—"

"I know," Mark said, interrupting her. He pounded his chest and lifted his right eyebrow. "But I'm a man, and a real man can take it."

Zoey laughed at his macho Tarzan impersonation. She'd spent only a little time with Mark, but already she knew he wasn't a chauvinist. Though he'd mentioned them only a few times, she knew he cared deeply for his mother and sister, and he'd treated her with the utmost respect since the first moment they met. *Although I'm pretty sure he was taken aback at the idea of a hundred-pound woman being his trainer.*

"Do you happen to have any recipes for people with high blood pressure?"

Mark's question broke Zoey from her thoughts. She huffed

and shook her head. "Yes. I found some last night, but I left them at my apartment."

"That's okay." Mark wrapped the towel behind his neck. "I was just going to take a quick shower here then run over to the grocery." He patted his temple with his index finger. "I'll just have to shop with my brain and not with my stomach."

"The first thing you need to do is stay away from the inner aisles. Try to buy as much as you can along the walls. That's where you'll find your fresh veggies and fruits, lean meats, and low-fat dairy products. And make a list. Try to get everything you need today so that you don't have to go back for a week, and—"

"Hello, Mark. I'm surprised to see you here." Zoey turned at the unfamiliar voice. "What a pleasant surprise." The thin, light-haired man gazed up and down her body in a way that made her want to ball her fist and smash his fake smile into his face. She loathed it when men treated women as objects, and no doubt a scowl twisted her face.

"Care to introduce me to your friend?" The words slipped through his teeth like honey, and yet repulsion overwhelmed her when the guy reached for her hand. She glanced at Mark, noting his tense posture and set jaw.

"Then I'll introduce myself." His much-too-soft hand wrapped around Zoey's. "I'm Kevin Fink. And you are?"

Zoey cleared her throat. Something about this man sent red flags waving through her mind. Call it a hunch, a sixth sense, whatever. When she was a girl, her daddy told her to trust her instincts. Her instincts warned her to stay clear of this one. Still, she had to be cordial. Trying to keep her tone friendly, she said, "I'm Zoey Coyle. I don't believe I've seen you here before."

More than she really saw it, she felt Mark move slightly away from her. The air seemed to seep from his chest when she introduced herself to Kevin.

"I just joined today." Kevin stepped closer, invading her personal space. "Believe me, you would have seen me before." His gaze traced her body again. "I would have made sure of it."

Disgusted, Zoey took a step back. She crossed her arms in front of her chest. He would not talk to her like that. Sure, he hadn't actually said anything inappropriate, but his gazes needed to be looking elsewhere. She opened her mouth to let him have it.

"I'll see you Monday, Zoey."

Mark's words stopped her. She looked at him, unsure what his tone and expression meant. He seemed angry, hurt, and embarrassed—all wrapped up into one big emotion.

He turned away from her, and Zoey stepped closer to him. "I wondered if you'd like me to go shopping with you."

Mark gazed into her eyes, a gentle look on his face; then his expression hardened and he looked away. "I think I'll go by myself."

He lifted his hand, and for a brief moment Zoey thought he might touch her cheek. She sucked in her breath, surprised at how much she wanted to feel his hand against her face. He lowered his arm. "Try to remember the recipes on Monday."

She nodded, unable to say anything. She watched as he made his way to the locker room. Something about the man—his kindness, his sweetness, she couldn't quite put her finger on it—drew her, and she wanted to spend more time with him.

"So, Zoey. . ."

She turned to face Kevin. The smile that stretched across his face reminded her of a villain about to get his way.

"I know a terrific deli a few blocks away."

"Thanks for the offer, Kevin. But I think I'll have to pass."

"Are you sure? They have the best chicken salad in all of Wilmington."

"I'm sure."

Zoey walked away from Kevin before he could ask her again. She could tell the guy wasn't used to taking no for an answer. And he was a good-looking guy. A lot of girls would probably be thrilled to go out with him, but she'd learned a long time ago that she had to base her choice of a mate on more than just looks. She needed a man of godly character.

Her mind drifted to Mark. He'd left so quickly when Kevin approached them. She thought he'd want her to go with him to the store. Several times during the session, she'd felt sure he was interested in her. *But I guess not.*

Zoey walked into the locker room, opened her locker, and pulled out her things. She'd wait until she got home to take a shower. She hefted her bag over her shoulder. *It wouldn't be the first time I was wrong about how a guy felt about me. Micah's proof that I'm not always the best judge of a man's motives. Which is why from now on, I do it God's way.*

She made her way out of the gym and toward her car. Her phone vibrated and she pulled it out of her bag. Seeing Brittany's name on the screen, she sighed. "Now if I could just get Brittany to do that, too."

five

Having showered and dressed at the gym, Mark pulled a comb from his bag and headed toward a mirror. He grimaced as he ran the prongs across the balding spot on top of his head. Logically, he knew most people didn't notice. He was a tall guy, and it was a small spot at the very top. But he knew it was there, and he hated it.

"Hey, buddy." Kevin's voice sounded from the other side of the room. Before Mark could respond, a towel snapped and he felt a sting against his hip.

Mark turned and grabbed the towel from Kevin's grip. "Watch out, Kev, or I'll have to pay you back."

"Go ahead." Kevin spread his arms and shuffled his feet. "If you can catch me."

Mark rolled his eyes and tossed the towel back at Kevin. "Maybe another time. I've got to get going."

Kevin moved closer, nudging Mark with his elbow. "Hot date?"

Mark thought of the text message he'd received from Maddy before he got in the shower, asking him to join her and their mother for dinner. If he got out of here quickly, he could spend about an hour with his mom and sister before he headed to Chris's for the first Boston Celtics game of the season. "Not exactly."

"Didn't think so." Kevin snorted, and Mark growled. Kevin rolled the towel then rested it on his shoulder. "But I do."

Mark tried to act uninterested, but his chest squeezed at the thought that Kevin Fink might have a date with Zoey.

I shouldn't have walked away. Why didn't I tell her she could get groceries with me?

He inwardly berated himself for his thoughts. Something had changed in him over the last several years. He'd become a Christian, and he loved the Lord with all that was in him. He strived to be a good son, brother, church member, and employee. He always did the right things, said the right things, even tried to think the right things, but something was missing. Something—

Kevin's whistle interrupted Mark's thoughts. "That red-headed trainer of yours is hot."

Bile rose in Mark's throat. "Is that who your date is with?"

"I wish." Kevin snorted again. "Nah. I asked one of the chunky girls in the aerobics class out. She'll probably cost me a fortune to feed, but who knows, maybe I'll—"

Mark raised his hand before Kevin could finish the sentence. He didn't want to hear another word from Kevin's lips. "Sorry, Kevin. I've got to get out of here."

Kevin shrugged. "Whatever." He turned toward the shower. "Hey, if you see a plump, dark-haired girl out there. . ." He touched his eyelid. "She's wearing some seriously dark green makeup. Tell her I'll be right out."

"Sure thing." Mark walked out of the locker room. A woman fitting Kevin's description sat in a chair outside the door. Her eyes brightened and she sat up straighter when she saw him walk through the door, until she realized he wasn't Kevin and she looked away.

I definitely don't attract the ladies anymore. Why would I ever think an amazingly gorgeous woman like Zoey would give me the time of day?

Starting to head toward the door, he glanced back at the woman who waited for Kevin. His conscience ate at him, as he knew his colleague had no decent intentions toward her.

Knowing the woman might decline, he exhaled as he turned back toward her. "Hi. I'm Mark." He extended his hand.

She shook it. "Myra. It's nice to meet you."

"I was wondering if you'd care to join me for a bite to eat."

The woman's face reddened, yet a full smile bowed her lips. "I'm sorry. I've already made plans."

What do I do? Kevin's less than honorable intentions raced through Mark's mind. Myra seemed like a sweet woman, and she was much younger than Mark had first realized. She probably didn't have the experience to spot the snake disguised as a man. *I can't lie.*

Even as the thought flashed through his mind, the words slipped from his lips. "Well, you see, Kevin is a colleague of mine."

The woman leaned closer.

"And—and something has come up at home."

Myra's expression fell.

"With his mother. And he asked me to tell you—"

"But my ride has already left." Myra glanced up at the clock. "She was heading to work, and now—" She pulled her cell phone out of her purse. "I'm not sure—"

"Why don't you let me take you to dinner?"

Myra bit her bottom lip. She took several deep breaths, her gaze shifting from the clock to her cell phone. "Okay. What did you say your name was?"

"Mark. Mark White." Part of him wished she'd said no. Her willingness to allow a complete stranger to take her to dinner needled at him. Kevin would not have treated this young lady well. He'd have taken advantage of her naiveté. Mark walked her to the door then opened it and motioned for her to go out first.

"Thanks, Mark." She smiled up at him, her expression entirely too trusting.

"No problem. So where would you like to go?"

❧

Zoey almost hit the car parked in front of her when she saw Mark walk out of the gym with another woman. It was true that Myra was sweet and kind, and Zoey admitted she was kind of cute, but Zoey had thought for sure that Mark was attracted to her. She gazed in the rearview mirror. *And I'm prettier and thinner and—*

She looked down and shook her head. *Forgive me for my superficial thinking, God.* She wanted so much not to worry about wearing the best clothes, sporting the cutest nails, getting the trendiest haircuts, working out for the greatest body. *It's like I'm not comfortable in my own skin. Ever since I got pregnant...*

Once upon a time, appearances were the last thing on Zoey's list of concerns. She didn't care how messy her hair was, how dingy her clothes looked. She bit the inside of her lip. Maybe her thinking wasn't exactly right. Maybe she'd always been worried about appearances, only back then she was obsessed with not looking good.

"What makes me think like this all the time, Lord?" she whispered as she carefully shifted her car in reverse and backed out of the parking space.

"I could blame it on the television or the Internet or magazines or books." Zoey tapped the top of the steering wheel. "I could say it's because appearances seem to be all men care about."

She turned down the road leading to her apartment. "But I know those things aren't the problem. Sure, they encourage the problem, but they're not the source." She parked the car, scooped up her bag, and walked toward the front door. "God, my value has to come from You, and You alone."

She rustled through her bag to find her keys. "Why I am always throwing the keys back in my bag after I park in front of the apartment, I'll never know."

Her mind drifted back to Mark. Prettier than Myra or not, Zoey inwardly admitted she'd wanted her new client to be interested in her. She wanted to get to know him better. She had a feeling, deep down in her gut, that he was a godly man. Not superficial. Not self-seeking. But a man of integrity.

Her fingers found her key chain, and she yanked the keys out of her bag then opened the door.

"Zoey!" Brittany's scream nearly ripped off the ceiling.

Zoey watched, horrified, as Neil moved away from her sister on the couch. Brittany wiped her mouth with the back of her hand. The lights were off, but nothing appeared to have happened. Yet.

"Time to go home, Neil." Zoey strolled into the apartment. She dropped her keys on the end table then walked toward the kitchen.

"You can't tell my guest what to do."

"Sure I can. You haven't paid your part of the rent for the last two months."

"That's because—"

Zoey raised her hands. "The reasons don't matter. I'm paying for the apartment." She pointed to her chest. "I'm asking Neil to leave."

Neil huffed and rolled his eyes at Zoey. "Whatever." He peered down at Brittany. The scowl on his face raised goose bumps on Zoey's skin. "You can make it up to me later."

He waltzed to the door, slamming it behind him. Zoey sighed at the relief she felt that he was gone.

"Why did you do that?" Brittany jumped off the couch and moved toward Zoey.

Zoey's heart fell as she noted two small dime-sized marks on each of Brittany's cheeks. She'd seen them before when Neil had grabbed her face, cupping her chin and embedding his middle finger and his thumb into her cheeks. "Where'd you get those bruises, Brittany?"

"What bruises?"

"The ones on your cheeks." Zoey gently touched the places.

Brittany's expression fell and she raced to the bathroom. Zoey knew they were fresh because the skin was still pink. She knew Brittany was checking to see how bad they were. "Just stay out of my life, Zoey."

"I'm worried about you. Neil's getting worse, and you seem to have more places—"

"You're wrong. You have no idea how good Neil is to me. Look in the kitchen. He brings me flowers. Takes me nice places. He loves me. You just judge him all the time. You all do."

Zoey frowned. "Who's 'you all'?"

"Mom. Harold. Everyone."

Zoey followed her sister into the bathroom. She leaned against the bathroom wall as Brittany started the shower. "Brittany, we all love you. We want what's best for you, and we're worried—"

"Neil says you don't. He says I should quit school and move in with him. Let him take care of me."

Zoey knew Brittany tried to sound strong, but Zoey detected the hint of fear in her tone. Taking a deep breath, Zoey knew if she blew up, she'd lose her sister's willingness to at least argue with her about it. "I hope you won't. You've wanted to be a teacher for as long as I can remember."

Brittany let out a slow breath. She looked into the shower stall, but Zoey saw the lone tear that slipped down her cheek.

Praying God would guide her words and soften Brittany's heart, she touched her sister's arm. "And I want you to stay here with me. I'll miss you if you leave."

Brittany swiped the tear away from her cheek. "Just leave me alone, okay?"

A retort begged to slip from Zoey's lips, but her spirit nudged her to be quiet. "Okay." On an impulse, she wrapped her younger sister, who was a good five inches taller than her, in a tight hug. "I love you, Brittany."

Brittany groaned, but she didn't push Zoey away.

Please, God. Please draw Brittany back to You.

❧

Mark's conscience ate at him as he tried to take another bite of the chicken salad wrap he'd ordered. Myra sat across from him chattering about gossip from her office. Not only was he fighting himself about the lie he'd told, but he was also trying to think of a good way to veer the topic away from her work grapevine.

My motive was pure. Mark inwardly tried to persuade himself against the guilt he felt. Kevin might have taken advantage of her.

The truth nudged at his heart. A lie never solved a problem or really protected someone. Myra believed he was interested in her, but he wasn't.

Tell her the truth.

Mark forced the bite down his throat then took a long drink of his lemon water. "Myra, I need to tell you something."

She flattened the napkin on her lap. "Well, sure. I've been yakking the whole time." She reached over and patted his hand. "I'm enjoying your company."

Heat raced up Mark's neck, and he feared it spilled across his cheeks. If the slight smile she gave him was any indication, he felt fairly confident his blush was noticeable and that she misconstrued it as attraction instead of guilt.

He cleared his throat. "I wasn't exactly honest with you."

She cocked her head to one side and furrowed her brow. "About what?"

He scratched the stubble at his jawline. "About Kevin not

being able to go out with you tonight."

A slight giggle slipped from her lips. "I know."

"You know?" Mark's heart seemed to shed half the pounds he was attempting to lose. Maybe Myra was smarter than he'd originally believed.

"I could tell you were fibbing about Kevin." She dabbed the corner of her mouth with her napkin then rested her elbows on the table and leaned closer to him. "I think it's really sweet that you wanted to go out with me so much. I'm really flattered."

Mark's heart sank. "It wasn't exactly like that."

She reached across the table and touched his hand. "It's okay. You don't have to be embarrassed."

Peering at her, he leaned back in his chair. "I'm sorry, Myra, but you're mistaken."

She frowned. "You mean you didn't want to go out with me?"

Slowly he shook his head. "You seem to be a really nice person, but no, I didn't want to go out with you as a date. We could be friends, but—"

She glared at him. "Then why didn't you just let me go out with Kevin?"

He swallowed. How could he say this without gossiping about his colleague? "He didn't have the best of intentions."

She squinted her eyes. "And you know this because. . ."

"Because he told me in the locker room."

She leaned back in her chair, studying him for several moments. "Let me get this straight. You acted like you were interested in me, convinced me to leave Kevin at the gym, because he didn't have the best of intentions. What were your intentions, Mark?"

"To protect you." *God, help me here. Show me what to say to convince her that I was trying to do the right thing.* Uncertainty filled him. Obviously, lying hadn't been the right thing.

"Why? You don't know me." She crossed her arms in front of

her chest. "I suppose you thought since Kevin's a thin, athletic man, he wouldn't be interested in a fuller-figured woman."

"I never said that."

"But you thought it."

"No. I didn't think it, but—"

"But what?"

God, help. "But Kevin did."

"How do you know what Kevin thought?"

Mark shook his head. "No. It's what he said."

Fury washed over Myra's features. Finally, she understood that Kevin was the villain, not Mark.

"How dare you?" She pushed her chair away from the table. "How dare you say that to me?"

Puzzled, Mark stood and reached across the table to encourage her to sit down. "I was trying to help you, Myra. I was afraid you wouldn't see through his words and that he'd talk you into—"

"So not only am I fat, but I'm an idiot." Myra pushed his hand away. "Thanks for dinner, Mark. I hope I never see you again."

Before Mark could respond, she turned and walked toward the door. The waiter approached and handed him the ticket. "Man, never tell a woman she's heavy." He looked at Myra as she walked out the door. "She was kinda cute."

Heat rushed through Mark. "I didn't say she was heavy." He pulled out his debit card and handed it to the man. "Could you take care of this quickly? She doesn't have a ride home."

The man clicked his tongue. "Don't make that woman walk."

"I won't."

It seemed forever before the waiter returned with his card. Mark signed the bill then rushed outside. He didn't spy Myra anywhere. Wishing he'd gotten her number, he headed toward his car. Maybe she'd realized she didn't have a ride home and gone to stand beside his car.

A familiar sports car pulled up beside him. "Hey, buddy."

Mark peered into Kevin's vehicle. He noticed Myra sat beside him. "Listen, Myra."

"I think you've said enough for one night." Kevin's voice sounded firm, but Mark caught the hint of teasing in his tone. "My gorgeous date and I are going to catch a movie then maybe a little dessert."

Kevin winked and sped away. Mark's stomach turned. He'd missed having dinner with his mom and sister and going to the store. *So much for trying to be a good Samaritan.* He blew out his breath then opened his car door and slipped inside. A true good Samaritan would have handled the situation quite differently, with a whole lot more up-front honesty.

Mark drove to Chris's house. Bruce's car was already in the driveway. Normally, Mark couldn't wait to dig into the boneless wings and blue cheese dressing, nachos and salsa, and whatever delicious dessert Chris's wife came up with. She always had game night pity on Bruce and Mark since they were still bachelors. But tonight his stomach still turned at what had transpired with Myra and Kevin. And he couldn't seem to get his mind off Zoey.

"Hey, man." Chris opened the front door and high-fived Mark. He pointed toward the car. "Saw your headlights pulling into the drive. I was afraid you were going to be late. Tip-off is in fifteen minutes."

Mark took off his jacket and hung it on the coatrack. "Just running a little late."

"Where you been?" asked Bruce.

Mark walked into the great room, grabbed a soft drink off the table, then plopped onto the couch. Popping open the can, he figured he'd earned the high-calorie, high-sugar beverage. "I joined a gym and had my second workout tonight."

"No way." Bruce leaned forward on the recliner and reached for Mark's biceps. "It'll take awhile to tone those babies up."

"Ha-ha." He took a long swig of the soft drink. "I just figured—"

"Does it have something to do with your doctor visit?" asked Chris.

Mark looked at the half-empty can in his hand. "Doc did tell me my blood pressure's a bit high."

"Maybe you don't need to be drinking that." Chris went into the kitchen then came back with a water bottle. He handed it to Mark. Feeling like a scolded boy, Mark took the drink and focused on the television. He'd known Chris since he was thirteen years old. Chris was there for him when he broke his leg, when his dad died. Chris knew. . . Mark stared at the water bottle and scowled. Sometimes, Chris knew too much.

six

Zoey tried to focus on the road and ignore her younger sister as Brittany huffed for what had to be the fiftieth time.

"I can't believe I let you talk me into this." Brittany growled and shifted in the passenger seat of Zoey's car.

"It's Cam's birthday, and Mom is fixing a big lunch for the whole family. Even Grandma and Grandpa are going to be there. You should be, too."

"I don't mind lunch, Zoey," Brittany grumbled. "I just don't want to go to church."

"It's an hour. You'll live."

"But we'll be back next week for Thanksgiving."

"You'll live."

Brittany didn't respond; she just continued to shuffle in her seat and growl intermittently. Zoey fumed over Brittany's self-centered attitude. If the activity didn't revolve around Neil, Brittany wanted nothing to do with it. Zoey couldn't believe that her sister, the one who'd spent all of high school enjoying basketball games, schoolwork, church events, and outings with friends, was now so wrapped up in her boyfriend that she couldn't focus, even for one afternoon, on something or someone else.

Brittany's cell phone beeped. Her sister read the incoming text and responded to it. Zoey watched as Brittany's expression fell and her body seemed to slump farther into the passenger seat.

"Was that Neil?"

Brittany didn't respond. Her gaze remained focused out the windshield.

Zoey's gut twisted in a knot. "He's mad, isn't he?"

Brittany pierced Zoey with an expression of fury. "What do you care?"

"I care about you, Brit." Zoey touched her younger sister's hand. "I hate seeing what he's doing to you."

Brittany didn't respond, and Zoey prayed her sister knew, deep down in her heart, that what Zoey said was true. The ride was silent, but Zoey's heart continued to plead for God's mercy toward her sister. *Please, God, show her.*

Brittany's cell phone beeped again, and again Brittany responded. With each mile, Zoey felt her sister's tension grow. Zoey's spirit groaned in intercessory prayer within her, and she continued her silent plea for help for her sister.

Finally at the church, she led Brittany into the sanctuary.

"Brittany. Zoey." Harold wrapped his arms around both of them, smashing them into each other. "I'm so happy you both made it."

Zoey patted his back. "I'm glad to be here. I've missed everyone."

Harold released his grip on Zoey but held tight to Brittany. He guided her away from the family. Zoey knew he would try to talk to Brittany. And though he never believed it, Harold always knew just what to say, or not to say, to help her and her sisters see things more clearly.

Candy grabbed Zoey in a hug. "I'm glad you came. For one afternoon I'll have someone older than three to talk to."

Zoey laughed as she squeezed her fifteen-year-old sister. "You're smitten with those twins and you know it."

Candy waved her hands in front of her. "I didn't say I don't love them. They're just exhausting. You'll see."

Zoey grinned when she saw her mom and twin sisters walk into the sanctuary. Candy leaned over and whispered, "That's the third time they've had to go to the bathroom since we got here. Fifteen minutes ago!"

Chuckling, Zoey walked toward her mom and scooped one of the girls into her arms. "How are you doing?" She touched the tip of Rebecca's nose. The twin giggled and shifted in Zoey's arms.

"I'm so glad you made it." Her mother wrapped her arms around Zoey. "You two live close enough that we should be able to see you once a week. It's been almost three. We want to see you more."

"I agree." Zoey hugged her mom then put Rebecca back on the ground and winked at Rachel. "Our schedules are so crazy."

Her mom waved her hand in the air. "I know. I know."

Zoey noted that her mom hadn't had a manicure in quite some time. Her hair seemed a little longer than Zoey knew she liked to wear it. Zoey clapped her hands. "You know what? We need to have Harold watch the twins one Saturday and you and Candy can drive up to Wilmington and we'll all get our nails done and our hair cut."

"That sounds like a lot of fun," Candy chimed in from several pews in front of them.

"We'll plan it over Thanksgiving break." Her mom motioned toward the front pews. "But I think it's time to get started. We need to have a seat."

"Where's Micah?"

Her mother smiled. "Cam and Sadie will be here. Grandma is with them. They'll come in right on time. Not a moment earlier."

Just as her mother said, Zoey didn't get to see her son until just before the service started. She knew she'd get to spend time with Micah after church. She peered down the pew, feeling such thankfulness to be sitting beside Harold, her mom, and all her sisters. In the row in front of them were her grandparents, Uncle Cam, Aunt Sadie, Ellie, and her precious Micah.

He's grown so much. Zoey longed to touch the back of his sandy-red hair. He looked like such a handsome fellow in his brown corduroy pants, blue button-down shirt, and blue and brown sweater vest. Sadie always dressed Micah in the most adorable clothes. He always looked clean. His hair was always trimmed. But beyond appearances, Zoey knew Sadie cared for her son as fervently as Zoey would have. In a matter of minutes, the singing and announcements would end and Micah and the other three- to five-year-old children would leave to go with their children's church leader.

"Can I have a pen, Mommy?" Micah's sweet voice echoed through the sanctuary while one of the deacons made announcements, causing a few of the couples around them to turn and look at him. They smiled, but Zoey watched as Cam whispered in Micah's ear. Probably telling him to be quiet.

Sadie handed a pen to the little guy, but Micah threw it down. "I no like that one."

This time Cam lifted Zoey's son onto his lap. She couldn't hear his words, but Zoey knew Cam was telling Micah he couldn't yell out during church.

Micah started to squeal, and Zoey reached into her purse, finding a blue and a red ink pen. She handed them over the pew toward Micah, but he was already angry and smacked them out of her hand.

"Okay, little man, we're going to talk in the foyer." Cam's voice was firm, and Micah's protests grew louder.

Zoey rummaged through her purse. Micah didn't need to get into trouble. In only a matter of moments, the music would begin and the congregation would sing with the music minister; Zoey was sure he'd quiet down then. She whispered to Cam, "I may have a purple one. Just a sec."

Cam peered at Zoey. "He can't be rewarded for throwing a fit."

"Purple pen. I want purple," her three-year-old screamed as Cam headed toward the door with the boy.

Zoey's heart ached. He was just a little boy. It was hard to sit still during church. She glanced at Brittany, who continued to text back and forth with Neil during the service. Even her nineteen-year-old sister wasn't behaving as she should. Zoey didn't want Micah to be in trouble. She twisted the strap of her purse. Maybe he would have sat still with her. She'd wanted to offer to hold him, but they'd come in a bit late.

Sadie reached over the pew and patted Zoey's hand. "He's okay," she whispered.

Zoey let out a breath, intellectually knowing that Micah was all right and that he couldn't throw a fit in church and that Cam had to take him into the foyer to quiet him. But her heart still hurt because her little boy had gotten into trouble. *I wouldn't want him to be rude and disrespectful, either.* She looked at Sadie and nodded, and the older woman winked before turning back in her seat.

Sadie had been a true gift from God. Having been through the pain of giving up a child for adoption, Sadie knew just what to say and do to ease Zoey's aching heart through the decision. After the death of Ellie's adoptive mom, Cam's first wife, God allowed Sadie a second chance at being Ellie's mom when she and Cam fell in love then married. *I won't be able to be Micah's mom, but I am able to be in his life,* and I know Cam and Sadie are good, loving parents to him.

She focused her attention back on the pastor. After the service, she would relish the afternoon with Micah and her family.

❧

Mark enjoyed the excitement in his young friend Tyler's voice as they approached Timothy's Riverfront Grille. Today Mark, his mom, and his sister would share lunch with a family they'd met during Maddy's cancer treatments. Afterward, they'd take a tour on the *Kalmar Nyckel*. Though he'd taken tours more times then he could count, Mark still enjoyed riding the historic boat. He found his anticipation swelling as he listened to the excitement in the ten-year-old's voice.

"What time do we set sail?" asked Tyler.

"Two o'clock." Mark smiled as he glanced at the boy in the rearview mirror.

"I can hardly wait." Tyler squirmed in his seat.

"You'll have to eat first," his mother responded from the seat beside him.

Sounding like they were still young teen girls, Maddy and her cancer-surviving friend, Trisha, giggled at some private joke from the backseat of Mark's mother's van. Mark never tired of the two girls' laughter, and every three or four months when the families took an outing together, Mark praised God anew that Maddy was healed.

"I'll eat, Mom," Tyler said. "We're almost there, aren't we?"

"Yep." Mark took one last turn then pulled into the parking lot of the restaurant. He turned off the vehicle and opened the door. "We're here."

"All right." Tyler jumped out of the van. He motioned for his sister and Maddy to get out. "Come on, girls. We've got to eat quick. What time did you say we set sail?"

Mark chuckled.

"We have two hours to eat, son. Let's enjoy our lunch first," Tyler's mom answered.

"Aah," Tyler whined, his expression drooping.

"How 'bout you ladies go get our table, and Tyler and I will walk over to the port for a few minutes," said Mark.

The boy's eyebrows lifted. "Could I, Mom?"

"I suppose," his mom responded. "But don't take long and don't drive Mark crazy."

"Okay." Tyler's face lit up; then he turned and raced toward the ship they'd ride that afternoon.

Mark followed quickly behind him, admitting he felt as anxious as his young friend. The cool November wind bit into his face, but Mark enjoyed the temperature, finding the harsh wind even more nostalgic as he and Tyler made their way toward the ship. He'd been no older than five the first time his dad took him for a ride on the *Kalmar Nyckel*. He loved the history of the ship, how it sailed to the New World from Sweden in 1638.

"Did you know that the people in Delaware's first permanent European settlement rode over on this ship?" Mark commented to Tyler.

Tyler looked up at Mark. "You tell me that every time we come."

Mark chuckled. "My dad used to tell me every time he brought me, too."

A stab of pain wrenched Mark's heart. Tyler was fatherless at the young age of ten. Not because of death, but because Trisha's illness had been too much for his dad, and he'd ditched his wife and two children. What a great guy. Mark inwardly fumed every time he thought of it. He missed his father fervently. Tyler had to deal with missing his dad as well as knowing the guy chose not to stay with them.

Mark tried to shake away the bitterness he felt toward the man he'd met only one time, and years ago at that. Each time he saw Tyler, he was reminded to pray for the boy's dad.

Mark focused on the mammoth ship before them. The hull was painted a light blue; the sails all hoisted high atop the foremast, main mast, and mizzen, awaiting the trip she'd make in only a couple of hours. Above the captain's quarters, an enormous American flag flew freely through the cool air. He noted the mermaids, castle, and fish intricately carved into the stern.

As a boy he'd envisioned sailing the ship as the captain, responsible for a whole crew of men. He dreamed of fighting off pirates and dangerous sea creatures. With his captain's hat placed firmly atop his head and his faithful plastic sword strapped against his waist, he would fight off the bad guys and critters who just happened to look a lot like his dad dressed up in blankets or paper or whatever they could find. And no matter how long Mark had wanted to, his dad would play with him.

He glanced at Tyler, wishing they didn't live over two hours away. *I'll be a better dad than Tyler's is.*

The thought brought a vision of Zoey to mind. Mark wondered if she wanted to have children. Not that he wanted to have children right now, but one day he would. And it was something he would need to look for in a prospective mate.

What am I thinking? He gazed down at his much-too-large midsection then remembered the balding spot atop his head. *I don't think my gorgeous trainer would consider me good date material. Even if she does have every quality I'm looking for: godly, kind, giving, pretty. I'm pretty sure I don't have all the qualities she's looking for.*

Mark cleared his throat and peered out over the river. He couldn't deny he'd love to take her with him on the ship, to share one of his favorite childhood memories with her.

He shook the thought away and focused on Tyler. "Have I ever bought you a captain's hat?"

Tyler's face fell. "Yeah, but Sammy sat on it and smashed it. The overgrown horse."

Mark laughed as he envisioned the enormous mastiff Tyler and his family owned. The dog was as sweet and docile as she could be, but she probably weighed every bit of one hundred forty pounds.

"Why don't I buy you another one?"

"Really?" Tyler looked up at Mark and straightened his shoulders. Excitement animated his features. "I'll be more careful this time. Won't put in on the couch. I'll keep it on my dresser."

"Sounds like a good deal to me." Mark patted the boy's shoulder. "We'll get it after we eat, but before the ship sets sail."

"All right." Tyler pumped his fist. "This is an awesome day."

Mark walked with Tyler toward the restaurant. A red-haired woman slipped into a building a few shops down the road. Thoughts of Zoey swirled through his mind anew. He thought of a red-haired urchin wearing a captain's hat and battling sea creatures. He shook his head. *I gotta think about something else.*

ॐ

Zoey's heart flipped as her young son padded down the hallway with one sock on and one off. He rubbed his eyes in one quick motion as he made his way straight to Sadie. Tightness squeezed Zoey's chest when Sadie lifted him into her lap and nestled her nose against Micah's neck. "Did you have a good nap, Micah?"

He wrapped his pudgy arms around Sadie's neck as he nodded.

Much of the time Micah acted younger than the twins, even though he was over a month older. Zoey knew Cam and Sadie were having him tested for auditory and sensory development and other stuff that Zoey didn't understand. It pained her to think she could have somehow caused Micah to have some kind of brain malfunction, even if it were mild. Sadie assured her that his delay most likely had nothing to do with the pregnancy, but Zoey couldn't help but feel responsible. She had been so young when she got pregnant, and she had no idea if Micah's biological dad had used any kinds of drugs or. . .

He is fearfully and wonderfully made.

Zoey inhaled a deep breath. *Thank You for the reminder, God. I can't worry about those things now.*

"I bet Zoey would like to play your memory game with you." Sadie looked at Zoey and smiled.

Zoey's chest swelled as her son jumped off Sadie's lap and raced toward the shelf that held the game. "Is he a bit young for it? I mean—is he ready?" Zoey asked her aunt.

Sadie nodded "Don't you worry, Zoey. That boy is smart as can be. Must be the genes."

Zoey couldn't help but grin. Anyone else would never fully understand the depth of pain involved in watching another woman be the mother to her biological child. But Sadie did, and she tried to make the relationship between Zoey and Micah easy and enjoyable. She wasn't threatened by Zoey and tried to include her. For that, Zoey would forever be grateful.

"Come here, Zoey." Micah grabbed her hand and guided her to an open spot in front of the television on the carpeted floor. He plopped down and pointed for her to sit beside him. After opening the box, he started to line the cards in rows, facedown. "Like this. You want to help?"

"Sure." Zoey joined her boy in forming a large square with the small cards. She glanced back at Sadie. "Are you sure he's old enough for this game?"

"Just play."

Zoey turned back toward Micah. "Okay. You go first."

She watched as Micah cocked his head to the left and then to the right. He selected a card in the far corner and turned it over. "The yellow duck," he squealed.

"You like the duck?"

Micah nodded, biting his lip with the entire row of his top teeth. He flipped over another card. It was a butterfly. He shrugged his shoulders. "No duck."

"No duck yet," Zoey replied. She selected one card then another. "No match for me, either."

They both took several more turns, and though neither had a match, Zoey smiled at the animation on Micah's face as the cards were turned. It was obvious which cards he liked the best, and Zoey loved watching his expressions.

"Duck!" Micah squealed when he turned over a card in the center of the square.

"Oh my." Zoey tapped her lip with her finger. "Where was the other one?" She looked at the four corners. She knew it was in one of them, and if she could remember which, she'd give Micah a hint. This game was too hard for him.

"I remember, Zoey." His pudgy little fingers reached for the card in the upper left corner. He flipped it and laughed. "Duck!" He scooped the cards into his hands and placed them beneath his leg. He pointed to his chest, a full smile framing his face. "I get to go again."

"Yes, you do."

Zoey watched as Micah turned another card. "Choo-choo! The train is my favorite," he squealed as he twisted his little body back and forth in excitement.

Zoey scanned the back of the cards. They'd seen the match to that one as well, but it was more toward the center. She just couldn't quite remember where.

Micah grabbed a card and flipped it over. His giggle pierced the air. "Choo-choo!" He scooped up both cards and shoved them under his leg as well. Looking at Zoey, he raised his eyebrows as he pointed to his chest. "I get to go again."

Zoey sat stunned as Micah made two more matches before

she had a chance to go again. She glanced over at Sadie, who shrugged her shoulders. "I told you. He's a pro."

Zoey flipped two cards again. No match for her, but before she got a chance to go again, Micah made two additional matches. She leaned over and rubbed Micah's head. "You're one smart boy."

Micah beamed as he stood up and pointed to his chest. "Smart boy." He settled back onto the carpet, being sure to push all his matches beneath his legs.

By the time the game ended, Micah had made every match but three sets, and Zoey was pretty sure he had let her take the butterfly set. He didn't seem to like those cards.

"Come color with me?" Micah grabbed Zoey's hand and led her toward the table.

Zoey's heart constricted when she looked at the clock. She'd have given anything to color with her son, but Brittany had to be at work in an hour and it would take them at least forty-five minutes to get home.

She glanced at her younger sister, who surprisingly hadn't been hounding Zoey about the time. She looked back down at Micah and scooped him up into her arms. "I wish I could, buddy, but Brit's gotta go to work."

He puckered his lip, and Zoey thought her heart would shatter.

"It's okay, Micah." Sadie lifted him out of Zoey's arms. "Give Zoey a kiss. She'll be back to see you soon."

He leaned over and placed a slobbery kiss on Zoey's lips. She yearned to take him back into her arms, but she knew she couldn't. Brittany needed to go, and Zoey needed to get out of there before she caved to her emotions and grabbed the boy and ran off.

After saying good-bye to their family, she and Brittany began their silent drive back to Wilmington. Brittany had been unusually quiet at the house today, but she'd also been less aggravated and grouchy. Zoey could only hope that was a good thing.

She also noted Brittany didn't text Neil the whole way back in the car. *That has to be a good thing, too. Wonder what Harold said to her at church.*

After dropping Brittany off at work, Zoey headed to the apartment. It was almost six when she walked in the door. Plopping down on the couch, the silence of the room wrapped itself around her and she remembered how good it felt to spend time with Micah.

Sadie's right. He's so very smart. He's going to be okay. Zoey kicked off her tennis shoes and grabbed the remote control. She didn't want to watch television. She missed Micah. She missed being able to be his mother.

She wanted to talk with someone. To tell someone how she felt, that she needed a friend to listen.

Mark popped into her mind. She liked him. Really, really liked him. But for all she knew he was dating Myra. But maybe he wasn't. *And I really, really like him.*

She pulled her cell phone out of her front jeans pocket. His number was right there. With the touch of a button she could call him.

Why not? What would it hurt?

She pushed the button, and his phone began to ring. Zoey's heart raced. A shiver raced down her spine. *But what am I going to say? He doesn't know about Micah. What am I going to do. . .just tell him all about having a kid just out of high school?*

Embarrassment washed over Zoey. She couldn't talk to Mark. She didn't know him well enough. He would think she was crazy, and if he was dating Myra—what would he think about his physical trainer calling him, especially if he already had a girlfriend?

She started to push the END button when Mark's voice sounded over the phone. "Hello."

Panic took her breath. Zoey forced her mouth open. "Sorry, Mark. Didn't mean to call you."

Before he could respond, Zoey shut her phone. She fell back against the couch. *I'm such a wimp.*

seven

Mark spent the entire day thinking about Zoey's call the night before. He'd been tempted several times to call her back, dreaming up various excuses to do so: reminding her to e-mail some recipes, asking her to join him on a grocery store run as she'd already offered, inviting her to dinner. He shook his head at the last thought. He had to quit thinking of being interested in Zoey. The idea of her reciprocating those feelings was preposterous. It was complete nonsense. *What do I have to offer her?*

Your faith. Your loyalty. Your kindness. Your love.

"Hey, man." Kevin walked up behind him and tapped his shoulder. Mark pushed his thoughts away and looked at his colleague. "I enjoyed my date the other night. Myra's quite the sweet little piglet."

Mark seethed at his colleague's disrespectful attitude toward women.

Kevin patted his trim stomach. "See ya at the gym." He headed toward the door. "Hey, are you working with your trainer tonight?"

Mark tried not to spit the answer through gritted teeth. "Yes."

Kevin shuffled his eyebrows. "All right."

"I thought you were dating Myra."

"I can't help what that woman thinks. I never asked her to be my girlfriend."

Mark turned back toward his office. He couldn't say anything. If he did, the words wouldn't bring honor to God. And if Kevin had any kind of response to the words, Mark might not be able to keep his fists from answering back. *God, I want to pray for that man. I want to want to see him come to know You. But Lord, I can't stand him.*

His spirit nudged at his heart. *You just keep bringing him before Me.*

Mark grabbed his keys off the desk and locked his office door. He waved to Betty. "See you tomorrow."

She scurried toward him. "It's been two weeks. So how much have you lost?"

"Seven pounds."

"Mark, that's wonderful. I've lost five. I joined an aerobics group at my church."

He twisted the keys between his fingers. "That's terrific, Betty. We're doing great."

He left the office and drove to the gym. Kevin was already there, and Mark could see him through the glass windows working out on a treadmill. Trying not to think about his colleague, Mark walked into the gym and headed toward the locker room. He had only five minutes before he was to meet Zoey. After leaving his stuff in his locker, he walked to the pool. Zoey was already swimming a lap toward him. The woman looked so graceful gliding through the water.

She saw him and pushed herself out of the pool in one motion. "Hey." The smile that bowed her lips nearly knocked him off his feet. It had only been two days since he'd seen her, but hearing her voice and seeing her smile validated how intensely he'd missed her.

"Hey."

"Sorry about that phone call." Zoey grabbed her hair and wrung out the water. "I didn't mean to call you."

"That's okay."

Mark's heart raced as she seemed to study him for several moments. She looked away from him, and Mark waited for her to tell him to get in the pool, but she didn't say a word. He walked toward the side.

"Wait." Zoey stopped him from jumping in. He looked over at her. She bit her bottom lip. "That's not true."

Mark frowned. "What's not true?"

"I did mean to call you." She shifted her weight from one foot to the other. "I needed someone to talk to, and—"

"You meant to call me?" Mark pointed to his chest. Zoey Coyle, his beautiful, sweet, wonderful trainer, had called him—on purpose?

"Yes." Zoey crossed her arms in front of her chest. "I mean, I shouldn't have. I saw you leave with Myra, and if you have a girlfriend—"

"Myra's not my girlfriend."

"Well, I offered to take you to the store; then I saw you leave with her, and. . ."

Mark almost fell over from what he was hearing. Was it possible Zoey could be interested in him? *What are you waiting for, Mark?* he chastised himself. "Would you like to go with me today?"

She shook her head. "I didn't mean to make you feel like you have to take me along to the store. . . ."

Mark placed his hand on hers. She looked up at him, and he drank in her chocolate brown eyes. Zoey was too beautiful for words. "I'd really like to go together."

"Okay."

A slight coloring of red made its way up her neck and to her cheeks. *She looks even more adorable.* The urge to trace her jaw to her lips nearly overwhelmed him. He wanted so much to kiss her.

She cleared her throat. "That doesn't mean I'm going easy on you tonight."

Mark smiled and tapped the end of her nose. "Of course not."

"Get in that pool."

Before he could respond, she pushed him in.

❧

Zoey Coyle, I cannot believe you practically threw yourself at the guy's feet. Zoey inwardly berated herself for what had to be the hundredth time since she'd pushed Mark into the pool.

She studied her client as he swam the length of the pool. A year ago, maybe as recently as a month ago, Zoey never would have believed she'd be attracted to Mark. He was cute, but more in a teddy bear way, and his receding hair made him appear a few, if not several, years older than he was. Still, something about him drew her.

Mark swam beside her. Sucking in deep breaths and blowing out his mouth, he grinned at her. "Okay, slave driver, what else do you have for me tonight?"

A thrill sped down Zoey's spine at the sweetness of his smile. His eyes shone with a kindness that Zoey didn't see in many men. In many people, for that matter. Her thoughts drifted to Harold, her sweet, unassuming, yet God-fearing stepfather. Mark's gaze reminded Zoey of him. The realization made her heart thump faster.

She clapped her hands, forcing her mind to focus on her job. "I think I've worked you hard enough tonight."

"You think?" Mark clumsily lifted himself out of the water. He grabbed the towel from the chair beside her. "I'm not sure my legs will move tomorrow."

"Sure they will. It was just a couple more laps than last time."

"A couple more laps, she says."

Zoey laughed as Mark wiped off his face.

"So do you mind if we grab a bite to eat before we head over to the store? I'm starving."

Zoey felt her cheeks warm at the mention of going to the store with him. Why couldn't she just have fibbed and told him that she hadn't meant to call him? Sometimes she wished she could ignore the Holy Spirit's prodding toward honesty, uprightness—godliness. *You know that's not true, God. I'm so thankful for our daily relationship.* She glanced at Mark, taking in the expectant look on his face and feeling embarrassed once again at having practically forced him to take her grocery shopping. *Oh, but Spirit, I do wish I just simply wouldn't have dialed his number last night.*

She shook her head. "Look, Mark, I really didn't mean for you to feel obligated—"

Mark raised his hand. "I'll take that as you're willing to stop by the deli a few blocks over before we go. And while we're there, I'd like you to tell me a few other places I can eat at, because I'm afraid I'm going to turn into a low-calorie sub sandwich if I have to eat there too many more times."

Zoey laughed, appreciating his attempt to ease her embarrassment. "Okay. I must admit I am a bit hungry. Get changed and I'll meet you in front of the locker room."

Mark saluted her. "It's a date."

"Well, not. . ."

Mark raised his eyebrows as if to challenge her. "It's official. It's a date."

Zoey felt her jaw drop as Mark walked past her and toward the locker room. If any other man had told her she was going on a date with him, Zoey would have set him straight before he had a chance to utter another sound, but Mark's challenge wasn't about control. It was a way to ease her discomfort, and she liked that.

❧

Mark watched as Zoey took another bite of turkey sandwich. She swallowed then pointed at him. "Another thing I've found is that you don't want to completely give up on all the foods you love." She picked up her lemon water and took a quick drink. "Give yourself one day a week to eat a hamburger or enjoy a dessert. Just watch the portion and only allow one day. Take Harold, for instance: His favorite dessert is chocolate cake—"

"Who's Harold?" Enjoying his time with Zoey, Mark allowed the question to slip out before thinking it through. She must have noted the jealous tone, because she grinned.

"My stepdad."

"So your mom and dad are divorced?"

"No." A pained expression crossed Zoey's face, and Mark regretted his question. "My dad died. . .about seven years ago."

"I'm sorry. My dad died ten years ago. He had a stroke. I think I may have told you that."

She nodded. "My dad was in an accident."

Their conversation halted, and Mark watched as Zoey dug through her bag of baked chips. It was obvious she'd been close to her dad. He understood her pain. He wondered about her stepdad. What did she think of him? Did she have any siblings? Was she close to her family? He wanted to know more about her, to know her history and what she wanted from life. He touched the top of her hand. "Tell me about your family."

She smiled. "Well, I have four sisters."

Mark almost choked on a bite of steamed veggies. "Four!"

Zoey laughed as she handed him a napkin. "That's right. I'm the oldest. My nineteen-year-old sister, Brittany, and I share an apartment. My fifteen-year-old sister, Candy, is still at home with Mom and Harold and my three-year-old twin sisters, Rebecca and Rachel."

"That's a houseful. So the twins' dad is Harold?"

Zoey nodded. "At first I hated Harold, but I kinda went through a hard time. . . ." Zoey frowned and scrunched her nose and mouth as if she'd just sucked on a lemon. "But Harold was really good to me during that time—encouraged and helped me—and I learned to trust him." Her gaze met Mark's and his heart thumped in his chest. "He's my second dad, and I love him."

"That's great. Do you get to see your family a lot?"

"Not as much as I'd like. They live forty-five minutes away, and with work and school—it's hard. I really miss Micah—"

"Micah?" Mark frowned, trying to remember if Zoey said she had a brother in that mass of sisters.

"He's my. . ." She bit her bottom lip and looked away. "My cousin—sorta." She gazed back at him. Her eyes seemed to search his face to see if she could truly trust him. He wanted to tell her she could trust him with anything, but the hesitancy in her expression held him back. She opened her mouth, then shut it, then opened it again. "Tell me about your family."

"I have a sister, Maddy, who's twenty-one."

"Like me?" Zoey's expression brightened and she pointed to her chest.

Mark couldn't help but smile. He loved the bubbly side of her personality. "Yes. And then there's my mom. And that's it."

"Are you close to your family?"

"Very." Mark folded his hands together. "My sister battled and defeated leukemia when I was a senior in high school. The same year my dad died. I've always felt responsible for taking care of my mom and sister."

"Wow. That's amazing that she's a cancer survivor." She twirled her fork between her fingers. "I can't imagine how hard it was to go through your dad's death and all your sister was dealing with."

"If it hadn't been for God—"

"I knew it!" Zoey yelled and clapped her hands, then covered her mouth. She raised her eyebrows and ducked her head, scanning the room to see who'd heard her outburst. "Sorry," she mumbled as she moved her hand. "It's just that I just knew you were a Christian. It was obvious in the way you talk, in the way you carry yourself. . ."

"Really?"

"Absolutely."

Mark studied Zoey as she picked up her sandwich and took a bite. "I think that's the best compliment anyone has ever given me."

She swallowed. "Then I'm glad I said it."

"For the record, I thought you were a Christian, too."

She nodded. "Thank you. I've spent the last four years trying to build my relationship with God after spending most of my high school years trying to rip it apart."

Mark watched Zoey. She was beautiful. A man couldn't help but notice her walk into a room. But having spent some time with her, Mark realized she was more beautiful than he'd originally imagined. He'd never again just "notice" her. Her godly beauty went too deep for that. "Zoey, I'm glad you agreed to have dinner with me tonight."

She huffed, crossing her arms in front of her chest. "If I recall correctly, I wasn't given a choice."

Her tone was filled with jest, and Mark grinned. "Then I'll have to force you to a movie this weekend as well."

Her expression fell, and Mark's gut clenched. *It was too*

much to ask. . . . I knew she wasn't really interested in me.

A verse from 1 Timothy wended its way into Mark's mind. "Physical training is of some value, but godliness has value for all things."

He sucked in his breath. Zoey hadn't accepted his offer to go to the movies, but he couldn't think about that. Not in the way he repeatedly had. Zoey's acceptance or rejection of his offer had nothing to do with his value as a person, as a man, as God's child. His value and worth came directly from the Father of the universe.

Mark needed to lose weight to be healthier. And of course he would have preferred to keep the thinning patch of hair on top of his head. But those things were superficial, having only some value. *I suppose the value of the hair would be to keep my scalp from burning in the summer.*

He bit back a chuckle at the thought. Sobering his thoughts, he knew his feelings of insecurity and inferiority due to his appearance were more than superficial; they were sinful. *God cares more about my relationship with Him than He does about my semi-bald head and soft center.*

He cleared his throat. "Of course, I won't force you to a movie, but I would love to take you to one."

Zoey's expression softened, and a full smile bowed her lips. Adorable dimples deepened in her cheeks. "I'd like that, but I'll be visiting my family for Thanksgiving."

"How about next weekend?"

Her eyebrows rose as she clapped her hands. "I've got an idea. Why don't you come over to my place first, and I'll fix you one of the dinner recipes I gave you."

"You gave me recipes?"

"Didn't I?" She smacked her forehead. "I forgot them in the car; then I spilled orange juice on them; then I forgot to make more copies." She shook her head. "Give me your e-mail address and I'll send them to you."

"That would be great." Mark jotted down the address on the back of a napkin. His heart nearly burst with excitement. She had said yes.

eight

Mark scooped a second helping of sweet potato casserole toward his plate. Thanksgiving dinner could end up being the downfall of his diet. Or maybe it wasn't Thanksgiving dinner; maybe it was that his mother was such a wonderful cook. Praying for willpower, he dropped only half of the spoonful onto his plate.

"Aren't you going to eat more than that, son?"

Mark looked at his mother, whose eyebrows furrowed into a line of surprise. "Mom, I'm really trying to stay on my diet."

She squinted her eyes, her expression questioning. "Why are you so determined, even through the holidays, to stay on your diet?"

Mark shoved a forkful of his favorite dish into his mouth. He was going to have to tell his mom about his blood pressure. Over the past few weeks, she'd become more and more suspicious of his eating habits, and he simply couldn't lie to her.

"Well. . ." Mark looked across the table, noting how his friend Bruce, a bachelor, leaned close to Maddy and whispered something in her ear. A flash of protective adrenaline shot through him as he realized his younger friend had paid more attention to Maddy than usual.

"Bruce?"

His friend looked at him, and Mark could see the genuine care for his sister in Bruce's gaze. Mark glanced at his sister and noticed that her gaze seemed to be pleading him not to say anything that would embarrass her. He swallowed back the desire to pummel any man who tried to make a move on his sister. Bruce was a good Christian man, and Mark had to come to grips with the fact that Maddy had grown up. Mark himself was falling for a woman his sister's age.

"Don't try to change the subject." His mother's determined tone interrupted his thoughts.

He glanced back at his mom. The hesitant gleam in her eyes made his heart race. It had been so hard to see his mother's anxiety ebb and flow in horrendous highs and lows when he was a teen. He couldn't tell her. Not yet. "I'm forty pounds overweight, Mom."

He hadn't lied in the least bit. He just didn't share the full reason he was so interested in losing weight right now.

His mother studied him for a long moment then released a slow sigh. "I guess I'll just have to trust you to God. He's taking care of you."

Mark grinned then sneaked a quick peek at his sister and Bruce, who were wrapped up in their own conversation. "Yes. He's taking care of all of us."

ಇ

Zoey mixed the mashed potatoes she'd made with garlic and skim milk, instead of whole milk and butter. Admittedly, she loved the fatty mashed potatoes smothered in margarine that her grandma made. But these were much healthier and still quite tasty. After grabbing a pot holder, she pulled the lemon chicken out of the oven. Not only did it smell wonderful, but at only 150 calories per chicken breast, it would be doubly delicious.

"I can't believe I let you talk me into this," Brittany whined as she walked into the kitchen. "I endured three whole days of family togetherness last weekend; now I'm spending

Friday night doing this." She smacked her hands against her thighs. Though pinned up on the sides, Brit's long brown hair flowed past her shoulders. Her sweater and jeans fit snugly against her tall, thin frame.

Zoey ignored Brittany's negative attitude. Zoey had enjoyed each moment with her family, especially with Micah. Much to her surprise, she'd been bubbling with excited anticipation all day about seeing Mark again. "You look really pretty, Brit." Zoey meant every word. Her sister was a beautiful young woman, despite the emptiness in her gaze. Today was the first time since she'd walked in on Brittany and Neil kissing that Zoey allowed him to come back to the apartment. A twinge of guilt sped up her spine because she hadn't told Mark that Brittany and her boyfriend would be joining them for dinner.

But Zoey didn't have a choice. Brittany was getting antsy to have Neil over, and Zoey didn't feel comfortable with it. When the idea to have him visit when Mark was there popped into Zoey's head, she just had to go with it. *Besides, Mark is a Christian, and he's my friend. If I need any help with Brittany and her boyfriend, he'll help me.*

She placed the pan of chicken on the stove. *Of course, I didn't really give him much of a choice, did I? Please, God, I pray nothing has to be said to Neil or Brittany tonight.*

Zoey shuddered at the thought. Brittany had become more withdrawn over the last few weeks. More secretive. She'd made fewer phone calls to their mom and hadn't answered Zoey's texts. Plus, she'd noticed a bruise on Brittany's arm a couple of days ago. A bruise that looked like someone had grabbed her arm and squeezed it. Brittany denied that Neil did it. She always denied it.

A long sigh slipped from Zoey's lips. *I've just got to keep praying.*

"How long is this dinner going to take?" Brittany whined as she grabbed the plates from the cupboard.

Zoey shrugged. "I don't know. I guess it depends on how much we enjoy each other's company."

"Great," Brittany huffed as she set the plates on the table then went back to the kitchen for silverware and napkins. "Shouldn't the guys be here by now?"

Zoey looked at the kitchen clock. "Yeah. They should. They're ten minutes late."

"Well, I hope they hurry. I'm starving."

❧

Mark berated himself as he opened his car door and headed toward Zoey's apartment. *I cannot believe I ate three pieces of that chocolate fudge.* Mrs. Adams was undoubtedly one of his favorite customers. Mid-eighties, white hair, twinkling eyes, ready smile. The woman looked as fragile as spun glass, but she loved to bring him treats. And her Christmas treats were simply too good to pass up. He growled as he trudged up the sidewalk. *How many calories are in a piece of fudge, anyway?* Mark raised his hand to knock on Zoey's door.

"Hey, are you lost?"

Mark turned at the unfamiliar voice. A hulking twenty-something guy stood behind him. A scowl marred his face, and he squinted his eyes. Widening his stance, the guy balled his fists against his thighs. "You're not here to see Brittany, are you?"

"Zoey's sister?"

"Yeah."

Fury seemed to spew from the overgrown hulk's ears. A primal urge to challenge the younger man swelled within Mark. He didn't appreciate the guy's accusatory tone or his stance. A retort made its way to Mark's lips as he fought the urge to ball up his own fists. Then recognition dawned on

Mark. "Aren't you one of the linebackers for Wilmington?"

The guy raised one side of his mouth in a half smile, half smirk. "Yeah."

The sudden change of thought allowed Mark to bite back a nasty comment and attempt to cool the tension. Mark extended his hand. "Hey, I'm Mark White. I used to play football a few years back. Got hurt and couldn't use my scholarship."

The guy's countenance softened as he shook Mark's hand. "That stinks. What position did you play?"

"Quarterback."

"Name's Neil Thurman. So you're here to see Zoey?"

Mark fought back the urge to shake his head. Neil wasn't worried that Mark might be here to see Brittany. The guy just wanted to pick a fight. "I am."

"Good. Maybe you can knock some sense into that girl."

Mark frowned at the younger man. His tone wasn't in jest. He meant it. Zoey's response when he said he would force her to the movies popped into his mind. Had Neil treated Brittany poorly? Mark crossed his arms in front of his chest. "A real man would never mistreat a woman."

Neil shook his head. "I didn't say mistreat her. I said knock some sense into her. There's a difference."

"So a guy should only hurt a woman when she deserves it?"

"That's right."

Mark took a step closer to Neil. "Wrong. A real man would never hurt a woman. A godly man would—"

"You have got to be kiddin' me." Neil pointed to his temple and twirled his index finger. "You're as crazy as Zoey." He swatted the air. "I'm not in the mood for this tonight. Tell Brittany I'll see her later."

Mark watched as Neil proceeded down the sidewalk and got back into his sports car. Without a second glance, he sped out of the parking area and onto the street. Mark shook away the twinge of guilt he felt at Brittany's boyfriend running off. No woman needed to deal with a man who thought so little of her. He'd never met Brittany, but she didn't need Neil Thurman in her life.

He turned to knock on the door when out of the corner of his eye he spotted a silver device on the ground. He picked it up. A cell phone. Must be Neil's. He shoved it into his coat pocket. He'd give it to Brittany once he got inside. He knocked on the door.

"Come on in." Zoey motioned him inside. Her apartment smelled like a mixture of lemons and cinnamon. Her warm smile lightened his mood. "Let me have your coat."

"Sure." Mark handed her his coat as he took in the varying light and dark chocolate colors of the room. Touches of deep green, as well as a small Christmas tree, accented the dark colors, and Mark found the room very soothing and comforting—the perfect place to relax and enjoy a football game or an afternoon nap.

"Did you happen to see Neil out there?" asked the tall, dark-haired woman he assumed to be Brittany.

"Uh—"

"Brittany, first meet the man!" Zoey exclaimed. She let out an exasperated sigh as she pointed at each of them. "Brittany, this is Mark White. Mark, my sister Brittany."

Mark extended his hand. "It's nice to meet you, Brittany."

"It's nice to meet you, too." Brittany blew out a long breath. "He's probably mad. Let's just go eat."

"Yes, I'm starved. Mark, I made lemon chicken and mashed potatoes, but these mashed potatoes are made with. . ."

Zoey's words started to jumble together as Mark thought of his encounter with Neil outside the door. *What do I do,*

God? Do I tell her?

He thought of the guy's phone stashed in his coat pocket. Scanning the room, he frowned. Where had Zoey put his coat? He didn't see it anywhere. He looked back at Brittany. Her face was drawn in an exaggerated frown. *Lord, she doesn't need to mess with Neil Thurman. I don't know anything about her, but I do know she needs Your protection from men like him.*

Mark peered at Zoey. She flitted around the room, making sure plates and silverware were straight and the glasses had ice in them. He could tell by her body language that she was trying to get Brittany not to think about Neil. The interaction tore at Mark's heart, and he found himself wanting to help Zoey protect Brittany.

He thought of Myra and how angry she had been with Mark when he lied about Kevin. *This isn't a lie. I just haven't had a chance to disclose the information.*

But Brittany asked me point-blank if I'd seen Neil.

But then Zoey cut me off before I could answer.

Mark rubbed his temple to stop the battle inside his head.

"Here. Have a seat." Zoey pointed to a chair at the dining room table.

As he sat, Zoey and Brittany also took their seats. Zoey extended her hands and looked at him. "Will you say our blessing?"

Mark watched Brittany roll her eyes as she took Zoey's hand in her own. She huffed as she extended her free hand toward him. He forced a grin as he took the sisters' hands in his own. His prayer stuttered out as he still warred over how to tell Brittany that Neil had come and gone. The tension between the sisters was as thick as the bowl of mashed potatoes Zoey had made.

He finished with an "Amen," and Brittany pulled back her

hand as if he'd smacked her. She slouched in her chair. "I just wish Neil would hurry up and get here."

"Well. . ."

Mark started to answer when Zoey nudged him with a large bowl. Her gaze begged him to comply with her request.

"Would you like some salad?"

"Sure."

Using the tongs, he heaped the lettuce-and-tomato salad onto his plate. "What kind of dressing do you have?"

"It's already in the salad. Try it. I think you'll like it."

An unfamiliar song sounded from another room. Mark looked up. Brittany had her phone in her hand. She hopped up from her seat. "That's Neil's ring tone!"

She turned and scowled at Zoey. "Why's it coming from your room?"

"What?" Zoey jumped up.

"Why is Neil's phone in your room?" Brittany squealed, tears filling her eyes.

"Ladies." Mark stood, trying to get their attention.

"Why would it be in my room? I don't want him in this apartment. Why would you let him in my room?" Zoey yelled back.

"Ladies," Mark tried again.

"I would never let him in your room," Brittany retorted.

Mark touched Zoey's arm. "Where is your room?"

Zoey peered at him. "What?"

"Neil's phone is in my coat pocket."

"What's it doing in your coat pocket?" Brittany swiped her eyes with the back of her hand.

Mark let out his breath. He watched as Zoey went to her room and brought his coat to him. "He dropped it, and I picked it up. I was going to give it to you when I walked in."

"But I asked you if you saw him outside. You said no."

Mark shook his head as he pulled the phone from his pocket and handed it to Brittany. "I didn't say no. I never had a chance to answer."

Brittany gripped the phone as she crossed her arms in front of her chest. "Well, where'd he go?"

Mark looked at Zoey. Her affection and fear for her younger sister were obvious. The intensity of her concern drew him even more to her. He would do whatever he had to do for the redhead who seemed to be capturing his heart. He gazed back at Brittany. "He left because I said I didn't appreciate him telling me that I should hit a woman to keep her in line."

Brittany squinted her eyes and shook her head. "He would never say that."

"Not those words. His words were that he hoped I could knock some sense into your sister."

"What?" Zoey placed her hand on her chest. "I knew it, Brittany. I knew he's been mistreating you."

Brittany turned her head and stared at the wall. "He meant that figuratively."

"Did he?" Mark reached out to touch Brittany's arm, but she flinched away from him. Her action sent a wave of nausea over him as he realized that Neil Thurman had made her afraid of a simple touch.

"You have no right. You don't even know me," Brittany wailed as she swiped a stream of tears from her eyes. She turned toward Zoey. "I want him to leave."

Mark turned to Zoey, whose expression revealed fear, uncertainty, sadness, and another emotion Mark couldn't quite decipher. He touched Zoey's hand. "Please call me if you need any help."

She barely nodded as Mark walked out the door. *God, help*

Neil Thurman. Guide him to Yourself. And guide Brittany away from him.

⁊⁊

Zoey spent most of the next week in prayer for her sister. She prayed in line at the grocery, while her clients lifted weights, as she walked from one class to another. During that time her feelings for Mark deepened. He'd been willing to stand up for her sister by telling her the truth, without sugarcoating it and without being unkind. It was a trait she'd seen and appreciated in Harold.

It had been a long day of classes. With finals only a week away, Zoey was overwhelmed by all the studying she had to do. *But right now I need a five-minute break.* She flopped into her desk chair and turned on her computer. Leaning back in her chair, she unlaced and pulled off her tennis shoes while it booted up. She'd see Mark tomorrow at training, but she couldn't help hoping he'd sent her an e-mail.

Finally ready, she opened her inbox. Just as she hoped, she had a message from Mark. She clicked the screen open with her mouse.

Twelve Pounds Down! screamed at her in bold green letters. She giggled as she scrolled down below the exclamatory message.

> *The hardest part was the beginning. But now that I have a routine, I think the weight will start coming off faster. Thanks for your help. Can't wait to see you tomorrow.*
>
> *Love,*
> *Mark*

Zoey felt a blush creep up her cheeks at the "Love, Mark" part. His first e-mail had simply said "Sincerely"; then it changed to "Yours truly." Now he signed his e-mails "Love." Deep down Zoey couldn't deny the thrill she felt each time he wrote it.

After a quick reply back to Mark, she scrolled further down her e-mail. Most of the messages were from various stores encouraging her to be a part of the latest sale. With every amount of restraint she could conjure, she deleted one after the other until she got to an e-mail from her aunt Sadie. She opened it and read the brief message. *Enjoy some pics of Micah and Ellie.*

Clicking on the attachment, Zoey felt her heart practically melt at the sight of Micah in his black pants, red-and-black-plaid button-up sweater, and red Christmas tie. The little tyke looked like such a big boy sitting on a white block with his legs crossed and his hands in his lap. The next picture was of him and Ellie cheek to cheek, hugging each other. They looked nothing alike, Ellie with her dark hair and eyes and Micah with his red hair and light blue eyes, but the two of them were inseparable. As much like biological siblings as two kids could get. A mixture of envy and thankfulness swelled within her. She was happy for Cam and Sadie, that they could have a second child in Micah. Happy for Ellie, that she could have a brother. And yet she hated missing so much of Micah's life.

She turned on her printer. Only two weeks until Christmas, and she still hadn't bought the first present. She glanced at the calendar above her computer. Payday was four days away. She could wait four days to buy something for Micah.

She printed the pictures. One of him leaning against a block with his chin resting in his chubby little hand was especially adorable.

She turned to her computer to turn it off when she noticed an ad from one of her favorite children's clothing stores at the Concord Mall. Her heart raced at the message indicating only twenty-four hours left for the biggest sale of the season. If she bought something today, she'd be able to save an additional 20 percent. She bit the inside of her lip as she tapped her fingernails against each other. Blowing out a long breath, she clicked on the Web site. As long as she didn't spend too much, she could turn around and pay off the expense when she got paid.

nine

Another week passed and it was time for Mark to go back to the doctor. He closed the bank account files he'd been working on and shut down the computer. Planning to stop by to see his mom and Maddy before the appointment, he'd taken half the day off this time.

Part of him dreaded returning to see Dr. Carr, fearing the prognosis might be the same or worse. The other part of him knew he had worked hard to lose weight and eat less fatty foods, so he hoped the visit would be positive. The memory of the chocolate chip cookies he'd eaten yesterday made its way through his mind.

The holiday season, filled with delicious festive foods, had worn down his discipline at times. It was true he'd stayed away from fatty fried foods, but the candies and the desserts—mmm, they were too good to pass up.

Didn't Zoey say I could pick a day of the week to eat some of the foods I like? Of course, he hadn't exactly picked a single day. After all, the candies didn't show up just one day of the week. He pushed the thought away. He'd worked extra hard at the gym on the nights he'd splurged with a piece of candy or two. Now wasn't the time to worry about how much he had eaten. He grabbed his coat from the rack and put it on.

"Time for the doctor visit, huh?"

Mark turned at the sound of Betty's voice. He took in her multicolored Christmas sweater as well as the jingle bells dangling from her ears. Her ready smile warmed his heart, and Mark gave her a quick hug. "Yep. So how much weight have you lost?"

"Ten pounds."

"Betty, that's wonderful."

"I wonder who's winning."

Mark couldn't help but grin at the excited gleam in her eyes. "Well, Barb seems to be doing a good job of weighing everyone each week."

"Yes, and she's going to post this month's results tomorrow." She clasped her hands together and nudged him with her shoulder. "Then we'll know who is our biggest competition."

Mark laughed, and Betty punched his arm. "Hey, I want to win that treadmill."

"Me, too, Betty." He looked at his watch. "But I'd better go. I'm meeting my mom and sister for lunch."

"Okay. I'll see you tomorrow."

Mark left the bank and drove to his mom's house. It had been less than a week since he'd visited her, but he still felt a wave of nostalgia wash over him as he pulled into the driveway of the home of his youth. Mom had never gotten rid of the basketball hoop that he and his dad had played one-on-one with every weekend. The privacy fence still had the perfect circular hole his dad had cut in it for Mark to practice precision with his football throws. Unnoticeable to most people, even the white vinyl still contained the various dings that he and his sister had made while doing one activity or another.

He noticed one of the strands of Christmas lights had fallen underneath the bay window. Before going inside, he fixed the lights and adjusted the nativity scene light set that must have been shifted by the wind. His mom still decorated the house for Christmas just as she had when he was a kid.

He loved that. He relished the memories of past holidays he'd shared with his family, especially before his dad died.

Maddy opened the door and pounced into him, almost knocking him off his feet. "Hey, big brother."

"Hey to you, too, twinkle toes."

Maddy laughed and lifted her hands above her head, intertwined her fingers, then twirled in the snow. "Does that mean you're going to watch me do *The Nutcracker* this year?"

"Don't you make me every year?"

Mark's mom had taken Maddy to see *The Nutcracker* play when Maddy was just six. She loved it so much that every year, even the year when she was the sickest, his little sister performed the play for their family. It didn't matter that Maddy had never taken a ballet lesson or that she was one of the clumsiest people Mark had ever known. It didn't even matter that the whole thing was atrocious and downright embarrassing. She still performed for them.

"Come on." She grabbed his arm. "Mom's got the potato soup ready."

His stomach growled of its own volition at the mention of his mom's homemade potato soup. He'd never tasted better. He followed his sister into the house. The succulent aroma nearly made him dizzy. Knowing he had his appointment today, he'd had only a banana and a small glass of juice for breakfast.

"Hi, son." His mom grabbed him in a bear hug as he walked through the front door. "We live in the same city and it seems like forever since I've seen you."

"Mom, I just saw you both less than a week ago, and you know I've been working out three days a week."

Maddy grabbed the waist of his pants and pulled on it. "And losing weight, it looks like."

"Maddy." He swatted at her like he did when they were

kids and she was pestering him for one thing or another.

"Still going to a gym. Still losing weight. What's all this about?" His mom pinched his cheek then stepped back, placed her hands on her hips, and stared at him. "Do you have a girlfriend?"

Mark felt heat rush up his neck. "What? No."

Maddy released the waist of his pants. "Tell the truth, big brother."

"I am telling the truth."

Maddy jumped in front of him and smashed his cheeks together with both of her hands. He swatted at her some more. Practically nose to nose, she squinted at him. "He doesn't have a girlfriend, Mom. But I think he likes someone."

"What?" Mark grabbed both of Maddy's wrists and gently pushed her away from him. "I came for lunch. Can't a man just visit his mom and sister without getting the third degree?"

His mother grabbed his hand and guided him to the table. She poured him a bowl of soup and set it on the table beside a ham sandwich. "So what's her name?"

"Mom. I said I didn't have a girlfriend."

"What's she look like?" Maddy sat beside him. She took a bite of ham sandwich and mumbled, "Where'd you meet her?"

Mark lowered his head. Dealing with these two women was impossible. He might as well not even try to keep his feelings for Zoey from them. "Her name is Zoey Coyle."

Maddy moved closer to him, and his mother slipped into the chair beside him. Maddy smiled. "What a cool name. How old is she?"

"Twenty-one."

"My age?" Maddy placed her hand on her chest.

"Isn't that a bit young?" asked his mother.

"I don't think so."

"Where'd you meet her?" asked Maddy.

"The gym."

"Is that why you joined the gym?" asked his mom.

"What does she look like?" asked Maddy.

Ignoring his mom's question, he replied, "Red hair, chocolate—I mean, brown eyes, small build."

"Oh, she sounds cute," said Maddy.

"Is she a Christian?" asked his mom.

"Yes."

"That's good." His mom leaned back in her chair. "Go ahead and eat, Mark. Your soup is getting cold."

Mark blew out a sigh of relief. For a few minutes anyway, the interrogation had ceased.

ﻬ

A thrill raced through Zoey when she picked up her ringing cell phone and saw Mark's name on the screen. With each passing day, she found herself more eager to see and spend time with him.

"I went to the doctor today."

The lilt in his voice assured her that the visit had gone well. "And?"

"Fifteen pounds! He's not taking me off medication yet, but he's not increasing the dose, either."

"That's terrific, Mark. I'm so happy for you."

"So what are you doing tonight?"

Zoey looked around her apartment at the dusty furniture, dirty hardwood floors, and pile of laundry trying to spew from the hall closet. "Nothing."

"Would you care to get dinner with me to celebrate? My treat, of course."

"Sure. What time?"

"Pick you up in an hour?"

Zoey looked down at her sweat-stained workout clothes. She forced her tone to stay light. "Sounds good."

Clicking off the phone, Zoey raced to the bathroom and started the shower. Was this a real date? Or was the invitation merely from a grateful client? If it was a date, what should she wear?

She jumped into the tub, allowing the warm water to soothe her tight muscles. *I do have that new red dress I bought for Christmas.* She shampooed and conditioned her hair and washed up in only a few minutes.

Should I wear my hair up or down? If Brittany was at the apartment, Zoey would let her help. It seemed like ages since Zoey had been on a real date. Of course, they were supposed to have gone to the movies after she fixed dinner the other night, but the Neil-and-Brittany saga had nixed that.

What is the matter with me? Zoey stopped and looked at herself in the mirror. She'd gone on several dates with some really great guys. She had no reason to be so worked up over a date with Mark.

"It's because I really like him." She whispered the truth aloud as she put on her makeup.

God, no matter how I feel about Mark, help me keep my mind focused on You.

She blow-dried and fixed her hair then slipped into the red dress. Her unease had settled and she determined to keep her mind and heart focused on God's will for her life. If Mark was part of God's will, then she would know.

The doorbell rang and she walked to the door. Taking a deep breath, she opened it and smiled at her date. Mark looked amazing in black pants, a deep green button-down shirt, and a matching tie.

"Wow." The single word spilled from his lips, and Zoey

could tell he thought she looked good as well. "Zoey, you're too beautiful."

She furrowed her brow. "Too beautiful?"

"Why would you ever go out with a guy like me?"

Heat warmed her cheeks. "Because you're a terrific guy." She grabbed his perfectly straight tie and straightened it. "And you're not too bad-looking yourself."

He offered her his arm. "Are you ready?"

She slipped her hand into the crook of his elbow. "I sure am."

Zoey felt like a princess all the way to the restaurant. Rarely did she have an opportunity to wear a nice dress, and even more uncommon was the elation she felt at having such a wonderful man beside her. One who, to her pleasure, was obviously very smitten with her appearance.

She raised her eyebrows and gawked at Mark when he pulled up to the Concordville Inn. "Have you ever been here?"

"Several times. You?"

Zoey shook her head.

Mark parked the car then rested his hand on top of hers. "Then it's the perfect place for a celebration."

"How so? It's your celebration and you've been here many times."

He shrugged. "I already know the food is delicious, and I'll get to watch you enjoy your first experience."

Zoey drank in the ambience of the restaurant, the town's lights, and the clear, crisp night. "This will definitely be my splurge night."

Mark chuckled. "Mine, too."

He guided her into the restaurant and toward the hostess stand. He had to have planned this. He already had reservations. Her mind spun at the various reasons why he might have already planned this evening. Did he plan to take someone else and the date fell through?

Trying to push away her restless thoughts, she walked through the brick-framed arch and gazed around the dining room. The top half of the walls were painted a rich taupe and adorned with contemporary artwork and rectangular light fixtures. Beautiful wood crown molding traced the perimeter of the walls and even sectioned off the ceiling. Ceiling lights added an additional glow to the bright white tablecloths covering each table. Rich chocolate brown and dark terra-cotta cushions graced the mahogany-framed chairs and booths. Bright red cloth napkins, a table light, and a single red carnation graced each table. Zoey had never been to a place so fancy.

The waitress guided them to their seating, and Zoey sat back in the booth and gazed at her date. Feeling a bit apprehensive at the elaborateness of the celebration, she traced the fanned napkin with the tip of her finger. "Congratulations, Mark. We're over a fourth of the way there."

"Thanks to you."

Trying to calm her nerves, she smiled, mentally telling herself to enjoy the place—and Mark. "I've been glad to help. You've been an easy client."

"I've tried."

She picked up the menu, surprised at the many foods the restaurant offered. "So what's good?"

"My favorite is the filet mignon and crab cakes."

"Mmm. I love filet mignon."

Mark didn't respond, and Zoey looked up at him. His dark eyes seemed to deepen, and a chill raced through Zoey at his intense gaze. "That dress is absolutely beautiful on you."

Zoey crossed her arms, rubbing her hands against her biceps to ward away the goose bumps. "Thanks. I guess it's my little gift to myself."

"Really?"

The intensity in his eyes didn't waver, and Zoey started bouncing her leg. It had been a long time since she'd felt attractive to someone, and she didn't know what to do with the nervous energy it evoked in her. "Yeah. I paid off one of my credit cards, and to celebrate I bought this dress." She took a sip of water then pointed to the dress. " 'Course, now this is on the card, but that's it. Nothing else."

Mark's intensity shifted to a frown. A twinge of guilt raced up Zoey's spine. It didn't make much sense to pay off a credit card then put something else on it to celebrate. In fact, it sounded downright ludicrous, even to her own ears. She shouldn't have bought this dress. And the compulsivity! She'd bought it for no real or good reason.

Mark picked up his cloth napkin and placed it in his lap. "Would you like some help with your credit cards?"

A hot trail of defensiveness sped through her. Moments ago he'd gazed at her as if she were the main course, and now he was going to lecture her about money? The heat of embarrassment tinged her cheeks. She knew she needed better control of her spending, but that wasn't any of Mark's business. "Excuse me?"

He shrugged his shoulders. "You've helped me. I could help you."

Zoey pursed her lips and glared at him. "Did I ask for your help?"

"Why are you being so defensive?" He pointed to the dress. "It's obvious you shouldn't have bought that outfit."

She sucked in her breath. "I like this dress. I—I thought you did, too."

"Yes, it's fine, but is it worth having more debt on your

credit card?" He reached across the table and grabbed her hand. "Zoey, I think you have a problem."

Zoey jerked her hand away from him. "How dare you?" Deep in her heart she knew he spoke the truth, but it wasn't his place to say such things to her. "I have a problem?" She pointed at herself then motioned toward him. "Let me ask you, Mark. How many times have you splurged already this week?"

"What?"

"You heard me. It's been six weeks. With the diet and exercise I have you on, you should have lost twenty pounds. So where are you cheating?"

Anger contorted his features, and he leaned toward her with gritted teeth. "I was offering to help you. I was not trying to challenge you."

"Were you? Were you really?"

"Mark, I cannot believe we ran into you here."

Zoey turned toward the thin sandy-haired woman beside them. Who was this? Was she his girlfriend, too? The man was just full of surprises tonight.

Mark turned toward the woman and gasped. "Maddy?"

"This has got to be Zoey," the young woman responded. She turned and motioned for an older woman to walk toward her.

"Mark!" the older woman exclaimed then placed her hand on her chest when she looked at Zoey. "And this must be Zoey."

A pained expression crossed Mark's face as he turned toward Zoey. The smile on his lips was obviously fake as he motioned toward the women. "Zoey, meet my mother and my sister."

ten

Mark wanted to crawl under the table when Maddy nudged Zoey and slipped into the booth beside her. His mother pushed him over as well. She extended her hand across the table. "Hi. I'm Sylvia. It's such a pleasure to meet you."

Zoey smiled. It was forced. Mark could see the daggers of anger her eyes shot at him. "I'm Zoey Coyle. It's nice to meet you."

"And I'm Maddy." His sister leaned closer to Zoey, wrapped her arm around Zoey's shoulder, and squeezed her.

Mark closed his eyes and shook his head. He loved his mother and sister, but the two of them were exasperating. They were busybodies—well, not exactly in a bad way most of the time. Most people thought they were easy to talk to and had the ability to make you feel better about yourself. And he knew they were intuitive, but at this moment he wished they would have taken all their wonderful qualities and sat on the other side of the room.

"Mom, sis, we've already ordered," Mark tried to explain, but his mother swatted away his words.

"Not a problem. We know what we want."

Maddy winked at Mark. "Maybe they want to eat alone, Mom."

Mark breathed a sigh of relief at his sister then glanced at Zoey. She bit the inside of her lip and glared at him. Before he could respond, his mother reached across the table and touched Zoey's hand. "Your dress is beautiful, dear."

Zoey cocked her head and blinked at Mark then smiled

toward his mother. "Thank you, Sylvia. Mark and I were just discussing my dress."

Maddy shuffled her eyebrows. "I bet he thinks you look really pretty." Her tone was teasing, and Mark knew she was about to say something that would embarrass him. "It looks beautiful with your red hair. Mark mentioned—"

Mark interrupted her. "Maddy, didn't you say that you might want to sit somewhere else?"

"I think it would be a treat to eat with your mom and sister, Mark." Placing one elbow on the table, Zoey rested her chin on the top of her fist and glared at him. "They'll be *nice, polite company.*"

Mark snarled at her while his mother and sister continued talking. The woman was incorrigible. Far too defensive. It was apparent she had a problem with using credit cards, and he only wanted to help her. He didn't want to get involved with a woman who couldn't control her spending. In his business, he'd seen many couples end up in financial ruin or even divorce court because one of the partners couldn't control his or her purchasing habits.

"He said you had a great shape." Maddy's comment broke him from his thoughts.

"I did not!" Mark stammered and looked at his sister.

Maddy rolled her eyes. "I didn't mean to make it sound like you were talking bad about her." She turned toward Zoey. "You know, like you're in shape. He said you all met at the gym."

"And you know," his mom chimed in, "the two of you looked absolutely adorable sitting across from each other."

Mark closed his eyes and shook his head. It would be better if he just ignored the conversation completely. There was no telling what his mom and sister would say next. There was no telling what they would tell Zoey he'd said, whether he'd said it or not.

I thought this would be a nice dinner between Zoey and me. It would have ended in a fight if Mom and Maddy hadn't shown up. Now it will most definitely end in embarrassment. God, this is a no-win situation.

≈

It had been a week since the so-called celebratory dinner with Mark. Since then she'd finished her class finals. A little over a week until Christmas—then she could visit her family and see Micah again. *Before I blink my eyes I'll be starting my last semester of college.* The notion seemed surreal, and Zoey could hardly believe how fast the time had gone.

Zoey grabbed a bag of rice puffs and plopped onto the couch across from Brittany. "So what are your plans for tonight?"

Brittany shrugged. "I thought I was scheduled to work, but I got my weeks mixed up."

"Not going out with Neil?" Zoey tried to keep her tone light. Things seemed to have grown more tense between Brittany and her boyfriend, and the last few days Zoey thought Brittany acted less willing to accept Neil's treatment.

She shook her head. "He has to work."

Zoey popped a rice puff into her mouth. "It's just you and me tonight, then."

"You're not going out with Mark?"

Zoey chewed the snack slowly then swallowed. She thought of the nearly silent workout she'd guided Mark through the day before. He still seemed upset about her "splurging" comments, and in truth, she was still miffed at his accusations about her spending. Even if they were true. She scrunched her nose. "Don't think that will be happening for a while."

Brittany curled her legs underneath her and leaned back in her chair. "What happened?"

It was the first time in weeks Brittany seemed interested in something outside of Neil Thurman. Zoey clung to the hope that her sister was beginning to see that her world didn't need to revolve around one person. *Oh Jesus, may she yearn for You. Is this a step closer?*

Zoey placed the snack bag on the end table, scooped up a couch throw pillow, and tucked it under her arms and against her chest. "Well, we went to dinner the other night."

"When you wore your new red dress."

"Yeah." Zoey cocked her head. "You saw it? I thought you were asleep when I got home."

Brittany shrugged. "I was in my bedroom, and Neil and I had just had a fight, and I wasn't asleep. . . ." She gazed at the far wall then looked back at Zoey. "Anyway, tell me about your date. You looked really great, by the way."

"Thanks." Zoey leaned farther into the couch, enjoying this moment with her sister. It had been too long since the two of them spent time talking. "Well, we kind of got into an argument about splurging."

"Splurging?"

"Yeah. I thought he liked my dress, but when I told him I'd put it on my credit card. . ." Zoey felt her cheeks heat up. Admitting to her sister that she had a problem with her credit cards was more humbling than she'd imagined, and saying the words out loud made it seem even more real. "He offered to help me stop using them."

"And?"

"And it made me mad, and I told him I knew he'd been splurging on food and that was why he hadn't lost as much weight as I thought he should have."

"Zoey!"

Guilt wended its way through Zoey. "Well, he *had* splurged more than he should have, and I didn't ask for his help—"

"But you need it. How much have you spent on Christmas?"

Zoey inwardly groaned. She didn't even want to think about it. She tried so hard not to spend too much money, but then some enticing sale would pop up in her e-mail, or she'd walk into a department store with a little cash in her pocket, determined to spend only the cash, but then she'd see a deal she couldn't pass up and she'd purchase more than she intended. *God, this isn't good. This isn't good at all. What is ruling my life?*

Well, it hasn't been Me lately.

The Spirit's nudging nearly forced Zoey to her knees. She had to do some serious soul-searching. She'd known for weeks, months even, that she had a problem with her spending, but saying the words aloud to her sister, who seemed to have much bigger problems—*Oh, sweet Jesus.*

Get the plank out of your own eye. The words she used to say and feel toward people who were quick to confront her during her teen years popped into her mind. It unnerved her that people would focus so quickly on her sins and not address their own. *Even if mine did need to be addressed.*

She looked at her sister. Brittany did need to get away from Neil, and Zoey would encourage her in every way possible to draw closer to her heavenly Father again. But Zoey had an issue she needed to take care of as well. Acknowledging her own failings, she nodded. "I do need help."

Zoey felt Brittany's stare for several minutes after she'd finally admitted aloud her credit card abuse. Brittany sat forward in her chair and grabbed Zoey's hand. "Can I pray for you?"

Taken aback by her sister's offer, she felt tears pool in her eyes. "Of course."

With their hands clasped together, Zoey sniffed back tears while her sister petitioned God on her behalf. The prayer was short and to the point, but it was sincere. Once she'd finished, Zoey wrapped her arms around Brittany's neck. "Thank you."

Brittany smiled. "As much praying as you've done for me in the last few weeks, it's the least I can do."

"How did you know I've been praying for you?"

Brittany giggled. "Sis, even when you're lying flat on the ground with your face smashed against the carpet, I can still make out my name."

Zoey chuckled and grabbed Brittany's arm. "Let's go grab a movie. Your treat."

"My treat?" Brittany pointed to herself.

"Yeah, I'm not using my credit card, and you still owe me money for rent."

"You got it." Brittany laughed. "Let me get my purse."

Within moments, Zoey was driving to the movie theater. Brittany turned the radio to a Christian station, and Zoey's heart nearly burst with excitement as they sang along with the music. Zoey pulled into the packed theater parking lot. She couldn't wipe the smile from her face as she walked with her sister toward the ticket booth. It had been too long since they'd enjoyed each other's company, and it was a welcome event.

Two couples stood in front of them in line. The biting December wind sent a chill through Zoey, but she couldn't deny she loved the two inches of snow on the ground. To her mind, it just made sense to have lots of snow for Christmas.

One of the couples moved into the theater, and out of the corner of Zoey's eye she noticed a familiar person. Glancing toward him, she gasped when she saw Neil with his arm draped around a small brunette. Zoey peered back at her sister to warn her, but Brittany's blanched expression was proof she had already seen her boyfriend.

"Let's go." Zoey looped her arm around Brittany's and turned her toward the car.

Neil looked over to them and scowled. He didn't even say a word to Brittany.

Zoey leaned toward her sister. "Did you two break up?"

"No."

"Oh." Zoey kept her tone low, attempting to keep her emotions in check. Surely her sister would not see her boyfriend out with another girl and still allow the guy to be her boyfriend. *Please, God, Brittany needs loose of Neil. She needs You.*

Zoey slipped into the driver's seat of her car as Brittany sat in the passenger's seat. Zoey turned the ignition, begging God to give her the right words to say.

Brittany touched Zoey's hand. "Don't worry anymore, sis. That was from God."

Zoey furrowed her eyebrows and looked at her sister. "What?"

Brittany swiped a tear from beneath her eye. "I've been asking God to help me know what to do about Neil. I'm miserable, but I just couldn't seem to break up with him. I needed help. It won't be so hard now."

As she said the last sentence, a dam of tears burst from her eyes, and Zoey leaned over and wrapped her arms around her little sister. "It still won't be easy, but He'll see you through. Trust Him."

Brittany sniffed and nodded. She sat up and buckled her seat belt. She looked at Zoey and smiled. "I know what I've got to do with my guy. What do you have to do with yours?"

Zoey scrunched her nose. "I suppose I know what I need to do with mine, too." She'd have to make a phone call when they got home.

&

Mark lifted his hands in surrender. "I gotta have a water break, guys."

"Hurry up, old man." Bruce dribbled the basketball between his legs. "We only have the gym for another thirty minutes."

"Give the guy a break," Chris huffed as he made his way toward his duffel bag. He unzipped it and rustled through it. "Water. Gotta have water."

Bruce laughed. "I don't know why I hang out with a bunch of old guys."

Mark took a long swig from his water bottle then wiped his forehead with the back of his arm. "If I remember right, it was only a moment ago I swiped the ball right out of your hands."

Bruce huffed and grinned. "That was luck."

Mark's cell phone rang. He pulled it out of his bag and read Zoey's name on the screen. Part of him wanted to toss the phone into the bag and head back onto the court. The other part was eager to hear her voice. He couldn't believe how much he'd missed her. He nodded toward his friends. "Be back in a minute." He walked into the lobby before he answered. "Hello."

"Hi, Mark."

Pleasure washed over him simply at the sound of her voice. "Hi."

"Listen." She paused, and already Mark detected the hesitation in her tone. "I need to apologize."

"Zoey—"

"No, listen. I was mean, and I'm sorry, and I do need help, and—"

A vision of Zoey in the red dress raced through his mind. "That dress was amazing on you. I didn't mean to make you feel like I didn't think—"

"I know. Will you help me come up with a budget I can live with?"

The opportunity to see Zoey quickened his pulse. "How 'bout tonight? In an hour?"

Zoey laughed. "I can hardly wait."

Zoey stared at the overwhelming pile of unwrapped Christmas presents on her bed. Even before she'd worked out a budget with Mark, the Spirit had nudged her to go through all the purchases she'd made. The nudging was confirmed when he suggested she take back as many items as she could.

"Whoa!" Brittany exclaimed. Her gaze traveled from the pile on the bed to the smaller pile on the floor. "Where did you even have room to stash all that stuff?"

Zoey shrugged. "I have no idea." She bit the inside of her lip. "I'm taking back all the stuff I bought on credit."

"Please tell me it's that pile." Brittany pointed to the items on the floor.

Zoey scrunched her nose and shook her head. She stared at all the gifts weighing down her bed. "I don't know how I'm going to do this. What will all those people think of me?"

"You're not going to worry about what other people think of you. You're going to do what God is guiding you to do; then you're going to listen to Him from here on out."

Zoey raised one eyebrow and turned to face her sister. She touched Brittany's forehead with the back of her hand. "Are you feeling well?"

Brittany giggled. "I know. I've not exactly been one to talk lately, but I'm changing my ways, and I'm going to help you change yours."

Zoey groaned as she watched her sister shove toys and clothes into various bags.

"Do you have all your receipts?"

"Of course. You know how proud I am of a good sale."

"Good." Brittany stood up and grabbed Zoey's hand. "Now go get me your credit cards, because you're not holding them in the store."

Zoey's heart lightened. "You're going to go with me?"

"Yes."

Zoey trudged into the living area and grabbed her credit cards out of the wallet in her purse. Thankfulness for her sister wrapped itself around her. She had no idea how she would make it through taking all those things back to the stores. Feeling very much like a five-year-old handing her mommy the toy that she wasn't old enough to play with, Zoey knew Brittany was right. Until she allowed God to have complete control of her spending habits, Zoey didn't need to hold on to her credit cards.

Give me a humble spirit, Lord. This is my weakness. You and I both know it. But Your scripture says Your power is made perfect in weakness. Help me to lean on You in this weakness that I may be strong.

❧

Zoey ran her fingers through her newly trimmed hair. She sat down and leaned back in the beauty shop chair beside her mother. Brittany, with her new short bob, sat down in an empty chair on the other side of their mom.

"You girls have no idea how much I needed this," Zoey's mom, Kelly, said as she handed a piece of aluminum foil up to her beautician. "I'm sorry you have to wait on me, but you girls don't have gray that has to be covered."

"We don't mind, Mom," Brittany said. She tilted her head as she looked at her reflection. "Do you really like my hair short?"

"It looks really good," said Kelly.

"It really does," added Zoey, "but then, you're beautiful. You'd look gorgeous if you buzzed it."

Brittany laughed. "I'm pretty sure I'd scare the guys off then."

"No, you wouldn't."

Kelly cleared her throat. "Still no Neil?"

Brittany bit her bottom lip. "No Neil."

"She's doing great," said Zoey. She wrapped her fingers around the arms of the vinyl chair, praying Brittany wouldn't become emotional. They'd had a wonderful afternoon. Zoey had really looked forward to their mother-daughters date, especially since they couldn't get three haircuts at the beauty parlor at the same time over Thanksgiving break.

"What about you?" Her mom focused her attention on Zoey.

"What about me?"

"Isn't there a guy—I believe you've mentioned him—"

"It's too bad Candy couldn't come with us. You'd think they wouldn't have practice so often during Christmas break."

Kelly shook her finger in the air, peering at Zoey through the mirror. "Don't try to change the subject, Zoey. What was the guy's name, Brittany?"

Zoey peeked at her sister. Her face was lit up brighter than the Christmas tree at the back of the shop.

"His name is Mark."

Her mom snapped her fingers. "Yes. That was it. What about him?"

Zoey blew out a breath. She twirled a strand of her hair between her fingers. What was Mark to her? She thought about him all the time. More than all the time. She even woke up thinking about him sometimes. At first she'd dismissed it as simply being interested in the well-being of one of her trainees, albeit one she really liked. Having dinner with him and feeling such fury when he offered her help had proven to her that her feelings toward him were definitely more than that of a trainer. She looked at her mom and shrugged. "I don't know, Mom."

Brittany huffed obnoxiously and rolled her eyes. "Puh-leaze, Zoey. Just admit you've fallen for him."

Hearing the words was like a smack in the face. Zoey

blinked at the impact of them, realizing the depth of their truth. She gazed at her reflection, then at her mom. "Brittany's right. I've fallen for him."

eleven

Mark hadn't seen Zoey in almost three weeks. He'd gotten the flu just before Christmas and was stuck in bed for several days. Then she'd gone to see her family for a week at Christmas. And as was the tradition every year, he took his mom and sister to northern New York to visit her sister and brother for the week of New Year's. Though he and Zoey weren't officially dating, he'd bought her a small present for Christmas that he'd wanted to give her. He couldn't help but admit that he'd hoped his New Year's kiss would come from her instead of his mother.

Can't change the past. I'm going to see her now. Mark looked at the small present sitting in the passenger's seat. The gift wasn't much, just a gift certificate to her favorite nail place and one to get her hair fixed. He figured he'd encourage her "no credit card" lifestyle and give her the money to do a few of the things he knew she enjoyed.

Parking the car, he placed the gift on the floor beneath the dashboard, hoping she'd agree to get a bite to eat with him after their workout session. His heart hammered in his chest as he made his way into the gym. He couldn't believe how much he'd missed her.

"Mark!" Zoey's squeal sounded from across the room. She raced toward him and wrapped her arms around his waist. "I'm so glad to see you."

Surprised and thrilled to feel Zoey's embrace, he placed his arms around her and pulled her closer. She fit perfectly in his embrace, her frame small yet strong. Though she'd obviously been at the gym for several hours, he could still smell a hint of her fruity shampoo. The whole gym could have shut down around them and he wouldn't have cared as long as Zoey stayed in his arms.

She broke away from him then punched his arm. "I've missed you so much."

Mark took in the two knotted ponytails at the top of her head, the style that made her appear younger than she already was. Her eyes gleamed with merriment and the deep dimples in her cheeks nearly screamed at him to lean down and kiss them. He fought off the urge and flicked one of the ponytails instead. "I've missed you, too."

She grabbed his waist. "You've lost some more weight."

He nodded. "My last weigh-in at work, I'd lost twenty-seven pounds."

She winked. "Talk about a hunk." She clamped her lips then released a long sigh. "I mean. . ."

Mark knew she must be as nervous about seeing him again as he was about seeing her. Zoey had a bubbly side, but this was a bit excessive—though he didn't mind. The notion of her missing him as much as he missed her filled his heart with hope. He wanted a relationship with Zoey. The time apart had proven to him that he wanted her in his life and wanted to get to know her better. He tried to ease her discomfort by putting his arm around her shoulder. "Getting the flu right before Christmas will sure help a guy to lose weight."

Zoey smiled. Her tone sobered as she looked toward the gym equipment. "Talking through e-mail is not as good as in person."

"I agree."

She guided him to a chair. "We have a few minutes before we need to start. Tell me about your holidays."

Mark told her about his Christmas and New Year's with his mom and sister. "I never apologized for them dropping in on us at the restaurant."

Zoey swatted the air. "Are you kidding? I think they're great." She twirled the string of her drawstring backpack. "I would love to meet them again."

Pleasure filled Mark. "I'd love that. So tell me about your Christmas."

Zoey's face brightened. "I've brought pictures." She opened her bag and pulled out an overstuffed package of photos. She pointed to each one, describing who the person was and what he or she was doing. Her cousin Micah was in almost every picture, and he couldn't count the number of pictures in which she was holding the boy.

"He looks a lot like you." Mark pointed to a picture of Micah opening one of his presents while he was sitting in Zoey's lap.

Zoey nodded. Her eyebrows rose. "Do you think so?" Her expression became unreadable, and Mark could tell she wanted to explain something to him.

"Hey, Mark, how were the holidays?"

Mark turned toward the sound of Kevin's voice. To his surprise, Kevin extended his hand. Mark shook it. "They were good. How about you?"

"Wonderful. I went to church with my parents."

Mark studied Kevin. Was there a change in his colleague? Though Mark spent most days wanting to pummel Kevin, he also deliberately tried to pray for the man. Mark knew without Christ his own ego ran a bit too big as well. "I'm really happy for you."

"Have we met?" Kevin offered his hand to Zoey. He nodded when she shook it. "Kevin Fink."

"I'm Zoey Coyle." She frowned and Mark knew she was

trying to figure out Kevin as well. "I believe we have met."

Kevin lifted his hand. "Oh, I'm sorry."

Zeke called Zoey's name and she turned and nodded to him. Kevin grinned at Mark, shuffled his eyebrows, then winked. Fury boiled within Mark. *That little snake. He's trying to wind his way around Zoey.*

Mark felt his fists ball at his sides. He took long breaths to keep from punching the man in the face. *One one-thousand, two one-thousand.* In his "before Christ" days, Mark wasn't exactly known for his ability to keep his cool. Even now he found it hard to stay calm.

Zoey turned back around and looked at Mark. "We'd better get started." She turned to Kevin. "It was nice to meet you again."

Kevin smiled, a smile so vile that Mark envisioned his fist uniting with Kevin's mouth and his teeth crashing to the floor. "Nice to meet you, too."

Zoey guided Mark toward the pool. "Your friend is nicer than I remember."

"He's not my friend." Mark's words came out with more vehemence than he intended. He wasn't angry with Zoey. But the gall of that man!

"Maybe you should try to be friends with him. Sounds like he's seeking Christ."

Mark closed his eyes and bit his lip so hard he feared he'd drawn blood. *God, I do pray for Kevin, but right now I just pray You'll help me not to pulverize him.*

⋅⋅⋅

Zoey let out a long breath. She was about to tell Mark about Micah when his friend or colleague or whoever the guy was walked up to them. She'd been so excited to see Mark. When she saw his car pull up in front of the gym, she thought she would literally jump out of her skin. She'd missed him more than she ever would have imagined possible.

She missed the way he raised one eyebrow at her whenever he was frustrated, the way he pursed his lips when he was lifting weights, even if the weights weren't too heavy. She missed the sound of his voice and the scent of his cologne. Never would she have believed she'd noticed so many things about him until she wasn't able to see, hear, and smell those things. She couldn't remember the last time she'd felt this way about a man, and in her quiet time, she knew God was pleased with her feelings for Mark.

Then Kevin interrupted their conversation. Ever since then, Mark was as grumpy and cantankerous as could be. He huffed when she asked him to do anything and growled at all her suggestions. She bent down to pick up a weight and handed it to him.

"I got it," he snapped.

Zoey placed her hands on her hips. "What is the matter with you?"

Mark scowled. "Nothing."

"Something is wrong, and I'd like to know what it is."

"Could we just train, please?"

"Fine." Zoey stepped back and allowed Mark to get his own weights. She didn't even tell him what he needed to do; after all, Mark White already knew everything.

She crossed her arms in front of her chest. No one could get under her skin as quickly as he could. It was like he had a magnetic force that drew the anger right out of her. The problem was he drew other emotions out as well.

A vision of Yoda fighting some nemesis in *Star Wars* popped into her mind. The Force is with Mark. She had always hated the movie when she was a kid, but it was one of her mom and dad's favorites. Something about it being a big deal when they were kids. It didn't matter; the memory brought a giggle to her lips, and Mark turned and glared at her.

She raised her arms in surrender. "I didn't do anything, Mark."

Mark looked away then back at her. "I know you didn't. I'm sorry, Zoey."

He stood and took her hand in his. Her heart raced and she wondered if he could feel her raging pulse through her fingertips. "I've been looking forward to seeing you all day, and I wondered—"

"Hey, is anyone using this machine?" Kevin walked up and pointed to the Universal.

Zoey looked at him and shook her head. She couldn't help but notice that Kevin was a really good-looking guy, and when he smiled, wow! The guy reminded her of a younger Brad Pitt. Not that the actor wasn't still drop-dead gorgeous.

Mark pulled his hand away from her and slumped back onto the bench. His anger was back. She realized it was geared toward Kevin, but she didn't understand why. The guy had acted like a real jerk the first time she met him, but he seemed different now. No one knew better than Zoey how much a person could change once God got hold of him or her.

She glanced at Mark. She'd wanted to tell him about Micah. It was important that he know about her past and how God had changed her. She wondered if he would still accept her. *He doesn't seem to be willing to give Kevin that chance, and he's known Kevin a lot longer than he's known me.*

The realization saddened her. Maybe all the pining she'd done for him while they were apart was in vain. Maybe she'd placed him on a pedestal without realizing it. She and Brittany had been such amazing encouragements to each other through her sister's breakup with Neil and Zoey's efforts to stop using credit cards. If she had been wrong about Mark, Zoey knew Brittany would be there to encourage her again.

"Hey, are you two dating?" Kevin's question interrupted her thoughts.

She looked at Mark. He snarled and stared at Kevin. Zoey waited for Mark to respond with an affirmative, or at least to say that he liked her and wanted to get to know her better. But he didn't. He just sat there, his gaze practically shooting fire at Kevin. If Kevin's question made Mark so mad, why didn't he respond?

The hurt she felt gave way to frustration. She looked at Kevin. "No. We're not dating."

"Hey, then, if it's all right with you, man"—Kevin glanced at Mark then looked back at her—"would you like to catch a bite to eat when you get off work?"

Zoey peered at Mark, wishing he would look at her, wishing he would see the hurt he'd caused her by not saying that they were thinking about dating or that he cared about her or something. But he never looked up. He simply stared at the dumbbell at his feet. Zoey peeked at Kevin. "Sure. That would be great."

❧

Mark could not believe Zoey agreed to get something to eat with Kevin. *It's just proof that women are blind.*

Or maybe it's proof that you need to step up and tell her how you really feel.

He smacked the top of the steering wheel. He was a wimp for not telling Zoey how much she meant to him. Now he sat in his car in the back of a parking lot watching her and one of the lowest men he knew eat dinner at their favorite deli.

Kevin was evidently telling her some funny story because he was flapping his arms like a goofy bird. Mark could barely see her smile, but he couldn't decipher if she was having a good time. *Maybe if I parked a little closer I could see better.* He shook his head. *No. Then they might see me.*

The absurdity of his thought smacked him in the face, and he rubbed his temples. "What am I doing here?" he whispered. "Am I some kind of crazy stalker?"

He turned the ignition and drove out of the parking lot. He made his way to his house then went inside. Walking into his bathroom, he turned on the cold water and splashed his face. He grabbed the towel from the rack and wiped off. Peering at his reflection, he whispered, "God, this is crazy."

Yes, it is. Your value comes from Me. Not from what you look like, what you used to look like, or what you'll look like in the future.

Humbled by the Spirit, Mark sat in his recliner and picked up his Bible. He turned to the scripture in 1 Timothy that God had shown him not too many weeks before. "For physical training is of some value, but godliness has value for all things"—he said the words aloud as a prayer to God and an audible reminder to himself—"holding promise for both the present life and the life to come."

Mark shut his Bible and quoted the verse repeatedly, aloud and in his mind. He drank in the meaning, allowing God to remind him of his worth through Christ and nothing else. After asking God to forgive him for his behavior toward Zoey, he went to his room and turned on his computer. He knew he couldn't say all he needed to say through e-mail, but he could start with an apology.

His cell phone rang. He looked at the caller ID. It was his mom. "Hey, Mom." He tried to sound cheerful even though he'd wanted Zoey to be the one calling him.

"Hi, Mark. I've been thinking a lot about you and Zoey, and I was wondering if you'd be willing to invite her over

Friday night for snacks and board games."

Mark grinned. His mom and sister loved board games. Something in him told him that Zoey would as well. And this would give him the perfect excuse to ask her out again. "Mom, I think that's a great idea."

"Terrific."

Mark could hear Maddy's whoops in the background. He was sure his sister was either on the other line or listening through his mother's phone.

"Okay. Unless I hear from you, we'll expect you at eight."

"Sounds good." Mark shut his phone then opened a new message window on his computer.

Zoey was already logged on. Excitement welled inside him. That meant she and Kevin hadn't stayed out very long at all. As quickly as his fingers would move, he typed an apology message to her. He kept it general, because he wanted to tell her how he really felt to her face.

He waited several minutes, but though she still appeared to be logged on, she didn't reply. Maybe she'd just stepped away from her computer or forgotten to log off.

Knowing she was still mad at him, and that she had every right to be, he went ahead and asked her to dinner and to his mom's house on Friday. *Maybe that will show her I'm truly sorry.*

Several minutes passed. Still no response. *It's okay.* Mark logged off the computer and shut it down. *I'll see if she responds by morning. If not, I'll give her a call. Lord, I pray I didn't wait too long.*

twelve

Zoey had just about had all she could take of Kevin Fink. The first time she met him she had thought he was a jerk, but then at the gym that afternoon, he'd seemed so nice. He'd even acted like he was interested in her faith. Now, however, his true self seemed to be making an appearance. He shared yet another crude joke, and she had to excuse herself from the table.

She headed to the back of the deli and into the restroom. After locking herself inside, she pulled her phone from her pocket. "That's funny. I have three missed calls from Brittany. I didn't even feel my phone vibrate."

She pushed the number and turned toward the mirror. Her hair was a wreck after a full day of work. She was tired and ready to go home. She never would have dreamed Kevin would want to stay at the deli this long.

"Zoey, it's about time you called," Brittany's voice sounded over the line.

"Sorry 'bout that. I didn't know you called. Listen, I need your help."

Zoey tilted her head and rested the phone between her ear and shoulder. She scoured through her purse for a brush or comb. She had no intention of trying to impress Kevin, but she didn't want the whole world to have to continue to look at the rat's nest on top of her head. After finding a hand-sized brush, she pulled out one ponytail then the other.

"First, I gotta tell you something. I've been using your computer because mine's not working right, and I forgot to log off your name—"

"Brittany, I told you not to do that. People think I'm online when I'm not." She worked the brush through her tangles.

"I know. Mark's instant-messaged you twice."

"What?" Zoey dropped the brush in the sink and grabbed the phone with her hand. "What did he say?"

"He wrote some big long apology about the way he acted at the gym. He said something about some guy Kevin and how he'd prayed for him for years and he didn't want you to get wrapped up with him."

Zoey huffed. "I figured that out on my own."

"He said he needs to talk to you in person."

"Well, did you respond?"

"No. What was I supposed to say? I felt horrible reading him spilling his guts out on the computer."

Zoey tapped her fingernails against the sink. "Well, why didn't you just log off?"

"I was trying, but I'd saved my paper to your computer and I couldn't get the printer to work fast enough. He asked you to his mom's house for a game night, too. Do you want me to respond now?"

"No." Zoey stared at her reflection in the mirror. An idea popped into her head. "I'm going to run over to his house."

"You've been to his house?"

"No. But I know his address from the gym."

"Hey, did you call me for something?"

"I'll tell you later. Bye, sis." Zoey shut the phone and put it back in her pocket. She finished brushing her hair and put it up in a single ponytail. Rummaging through her purse, she found a tube of lip gloss, mascara, and some blush. She wet and dried her face then applied the makeup she had with her. Satisfied with her appearance, she walked out of the bathroom.

No surprise to her, Kevin had scooted his chair beside an attractive woman who sat at the table adjacent to theirs. When he saw her, he smiled and moved his chair back in one swift move. "I was beginning to wonder if you fell in." He spread his arms wide. "But I can see you were just freshening up for me."

Zoey bit back a growl. "Thanks for the sandwich, Kevin, but I have to go."

"But you didn't finish your food."

"I'm sorry."

She'd reached the door when her conscience got the better of her. She turned to apologize for her curt behavior, but Kevin had already moved beside the woman at the other table. Zoey almost laughed out loud. *Wow! Now I know why Mark got so upset each time Kevin talked to us.*

She walked out the door and slid into her car. Turning the ignition, she glanced at the clock. It was only eight. Not too late to visit Mark. She knew just where he lived since she hadn't been able to resist driving by his house one time while he was gone to New York with his mom and sister.

God, I want to be honest with him about the way I feel, about Micah. He's someone I'd be willing to take home to meet Mom and Harold and Micah. In fact, that would be a great idea.

She pulled into the driveway behind his car. Fear wrapped around her heart as she looked at the two-story town house. She gripped the car door handle. *Maybe I shouldn't be here. He's not expecting me, probably doesn't want to see me.*

But Brittany said he wrote a long apology message.

Mustering all the courage she could find, she stepped out of the car and walked to the front door. She stood there several moments before balling her hand into a fist, ready to knock on the door. *Oh boy. Oh boy. I don't think I can do this.*

She couldn't just stand there all night. What would his

neighbors think? She clutched her fist with her other hand. It was cold outside, colder than it had been in days, and already her nose and cheeks felt the effect of the night wind. She should have worn her mittens and put on some earmuffs, especially if she was going to stand outside in the elements all evening. Taking another deep breath, she balled her fist again to knock.

The door opened, and Zoey squealed and jumped back. Mark gasped then pulled the door open all the way. "Zoey? What are you doing here?"

Zoey flattened her palm against her speeding heart. She took several breaths to ensure she hadn't just had a heart attack. "I wanted to talk with you."

He motioned her inside. "Come on in. You look like you're freezing to death. How long have you been out there?"

"Too long."

"Let me have your coat." Zoey inhaled the scent of Mark's home. It didn't smell like candles or even his cologne. It had more of a woodsy scent. As she scanned the room, taking in the deep green and brown colors of his furnishings, she was surprised at the similarity of their decorating tastes. On the far end table she spied a reed diffuser. *Sandalwood. That's what the smell is.*

"Come on, Zoey." He gently grabbed her arm and led her to an oversized chair. "Have a seat. Would you like a cup of coffee?"

Zoey nodded. "Actually, I think I would."

"Okay. I'll be right back."

Zoey stared at Mark's oversized flat-screen television as well as the Wii game station beneath it. She never would have figured Mark to be a Wii guy. But why wouldn't he be? The few times she'd had the opportunity to play one of the games, she'd really enjoyed it. Even if she was terrible.

"Do you like anything in your coffee?" Mark called from the kitchen.

"Just cream. Thanks."

Mark walked into the living room and handed her the coffee. He placed his cup on the end table and sat in the chair across from her. He clasped his hands in front of him. He seemed as nervous as she felt. "So you read my messages?" His voice was low and hesitant.

"Actually, no." She placed her coffee on the table beside her. "Brittany was on my computer, and I was still with Kevin."

"Oh." He nodded and Zoey noticed a bright red streak cover his neck. He cleared his throat. "Well, what I said—"

"Kevin's not a very nice guy."

Mark shook his head. "I'm afraid he's not."

"You didn't know how to warn me."

"I didn't."

Zoey leaned forward in the chair. "What I need to know is why you would want to warn me. Is it just because we're friends?"

Mark shifted in his chair as he shook his head. "No. It's not."

Zoey moved closer to the edge of her seat. "Does that mean you. . ." How did she say it without sounding like she was fifteen again? *Oh, who cares? Just be honest, Zoey.* "You like me?"

Mark got up and walked toward the bookcase beside his television. He fingered the tops of several books. "Look at me, Zoey. I'm six years older than you. I've still got some weight to lose."

"Barely, and why would that matter?"

"I'm even getting a bald spot on the top of my head."

Zoey scrunched up her nose, inwardly giggling at the thought. "You are?"

He turned around and walked to her. Taking her hands in

his, he guided her to her feet. Her heart sped up at the look in his eye. The intensity she remembered from the inn had returned to his gaze, sending chills up and down her arms. "Zoey, I'm absolutely crazy about you."

"Really?"

He released her hands and wiped his face with the palm of his hand. "The three weeks I couldn't see you were the longest weeks of my life. I thought I was going nuts. Every time I saw a red-haired woman I thought of you. I watched her until I knew she wasn't you."

A giggle swelled within her throat until she couldn't contain it any longer. "I'm crazy about you, too."

Before she could utter another word, Mark wrapped his arms around her and pressed his lips against her forehead. She hugged him around his waist. "It's been a long time since I felt this way."

"Me, too."

Mark held her for several moments. Zoey relished his scent, wondering if he would cup her chin and kiss her lips. She wanted him to, but she enjoyed the warmth of his embrace as well.

He kissed the top of her head again. "Did Brittany tell you about my mom inviting us to play board games on Friday?"

Zoey nodded. "I can't wait."

Mark released her. He touched the side of her cheek with the back of his finger. "How could a woman as beautiful as you give me a second glance?"

She bit the inside of her lip. His sweet tone and gentle touch overwhelmed her. Even more, the fact that he loved her Jesus and wanted to serve Him thrilled her to the core of her being. God was blessing her despite the mistakes she'd made in the past.

I need to tell him about Micah. Her stomach twisted with

fear that he would be upset and reject her when she told him the truth. Not only was she not a virgin, but she'd also carried and birthed a child and given that child up for adoption. But she had to tell him. She'd have to face whatever response he had. "Mark—"

"Zoey, have you ever played a Wii?"

Zoey glanced up at Mark. The challenging glint in his eye made her smile. "Only a few times. I'm not very good."

"My mom bought this for me for Christmas, and I'm addicted to it." He patted his belly. "It's good for the weight loss, too." He held a control out to her. "Wanna try?"

Zoey laughed out loud at the childish expression on Mark's face. She could tell him about Micah on Friday. For now, she was going to learn how to play a Wii.

❧

Mark couldn't mask his happiness as he walked into the bank the following morning. He didn't even want to hide it. Each day it seemed his pants fit looser. Today, he'd had to tighten his belt another notch. And tonight he'd see Zoey again at the gym, and probably enjoy dinner with her afterward. Life simply couldn't get any better.

He walked into his office, sat in his leather chair, then turned on the computer. Waiting for the system to boot, he arranged his phone messages in order of importance. He glanced at the calendar. He could hardly believe January was half over. Turning toward his computer, he clicked on his e-mail. He opened a message from Kevin gloating about what a great time he'd had with Zoey.

Frustrated, he pushed away from his computer and leaned back in the chair. If anyone could make his blood pressure rise, Kevin Fink could. *He's starting in on me awfully early. He's not usually even here yet.* Mark stood and paced in front of his desk. *I know good and well he didn't have a blast with Zoey, because she spent most of the evening with me.*

The man seemed to thrive on getting under Mark's skin. It was like his mission in life. Angry retorts buzzed through his mind. Normally Mark tried to count down from the fury, but this morning he'd had it. *There comes a time when a man just needs to speak his mind.*

Mark sat back down at his desk. In a matter of moments, he wrote a reply calling Kevin out on his little exaggeration. But Mark's frustration didn't stop there. He continued to type another five lines or so explaining that he was no longer going to take Kevin's manipulative actions. Not wanting the chance to calm down and change his mind, Mark sent the e-mail without reading over what he'd written.

I don't even care if it's full of typos or if the sentences don't make complete sense. Enough is enough.

With a huff, Mark stood again. This time he walked out of his office and headed to the coffeepot. Pouring a small cup, he peered into Kevin's office. The lights weren't on. What did the man do? Send the e-mail from his house? *What is it about me that makes him feel so threatened?*

He headed back to his office. He was done messing with Kevin. Praying for the man for the past five years hadn't changed him at all. If he said anything else today, Mark planned to put him in his place.

The front door opened and Betty walked inside. She saw Mark and started to cry. Mark walked forward and put his arm around her shoulder. "Betty, what's wrong?"

"Oh Mark, it's awful," she wailed.

Mark guided her to a cushiony chair in the lobby. He pulled a tissue from the box on the counter and handed it to his manager. "Betty, what is it?"

"There's been an accident."

"What kind of accident?"

Betty dabbed her eyes then blew her nose. "A car accident. And Kevin—" Her chest heaved and more tears rolled down her cheeks.

His heart sunk as a feeling of doom washed over him. "What about Kevin?"

"He's dead."

❧

Two days later Mark sat in a metal folding chair staring at a casket draped with an arrangement of blue and white flowers. Zoey sat beside him, listening to the preacher talk about Kevin's life. It was a generic eulogy—one he knew his own pastor struggled through when the person who'd passed away didn't know Christ as his or her Savior. He glanced around the room filled with Kevin's family, their colleagues, and several of the bank's patrons before focusing on the casket again. Someone near him murmured, "Such a senseless tragedy."

Mark felt empty, like someone had taken out his insides and hidden them from him. He and Betty had been given the task of going through Kevin's files and e-mails. The last message he sent Kevin stuck in his mind. The anger Mark had felt at that moment had been pointless. It would not have changed Kevin's behavior and attitude, but it did change Mark—for the worse.

Zoey squeezed his hand and peered up at him. "Are you okay?"

Mark inhaled. "I will be. You know I've spent five years praying for him."

"I know."

Mark looked down at their intertwined hands. "Didn't do much good, did it?"

"Of course it did. It did you good." She squeezed his hand. "You can't control others' responses."

God, I should have controlled my response. I was so angry

with him. Sure, I prayed for him, but how many times did I respond to his comments too sharply and too quickly? How many times did he see more of the fleshly Mark White and less of You?

Guilt ate away at him as memory after memory of retorts flooded his mind. He wished he could take them all back, that he could have been a better witness to Kevin.

The preacher finished the eulogy and Mark took his place as a pallbearer with a couple of his other colleagues and a few of Kevin's friends from college. They waited as Kevin's father and mother said their last good-byes. Mark knew Kevin's father's pale expression and mother's tearstained face would haunt him for the next several months. The whole thing still seemed surreal—until the casket was closed and Mark lifted his portion of the weight. It was heavier than he thought.

God. The silent plea slipped through his mind. He remembered his father's death and burial. The pain attacked him afresh and piled onto the guilt he felt over Kevin. His dad had been a good man. Mark had nothing to regret in terms of his relationship with his father.

But with Kevin? Even though the man was dead, Mark still didn't like him. What did that make him? How could he have genuinely prayed for a man he didn't like? *Maybe I never did pray for him from my heart, Lord. Were my petitions shallow? Did I really want him to change, to come to know You, or was I just uttering words in my mind because I knew I should?*

Kevin's behavior toward women practically mirrored the way Mark treated girls when he was a teen. Mark had been selfish and egotistical. The memories embarrassed and saddened him. When he watched Kevin's actions, he felt as if his own sins were being rehashed and shoved in his face anew. *Did he ever have the opportunity to see You in me, or was I still so self-absorbed, stewing over how his actions made me feel, that I couldn't see clearly to be a living testimony? Was I just worried about me? Did I really want him to change?*

You did.

Mark pushed away the Spirit's nudging. He should have been a better witness. The grave site, the burial, the rest of the funeral all passed in a blur. With the last song sung and the last prayer uttered, family and friends made their way to their vehicles, but Mark stood back watching Kevin's parents. His mother, almost too weak to stand, clung to his father's arm and shoulder. The man stood stoically, obviously trying to be strong for his wife, but Mark could see that his jaw was shaking and that at any moment tears would flow freely down the older man's cheeks.

Mark remembered how hard it had been to bury his father. How awful would it be to bury a child? He couldn't fathom it. Zoey walked up beside him and looped her arm around his. "I'm sorry, Mark."

Mark couldn't look at her. The guilt he felt gnawed at him. "Don't feel sorry for me. I didn't even like him."

"That's not true." Her gaze penetrated him. "If you didn't like him, then why do you feel so sad?"

"Because I should have liked him."

"No, Mark. You did care about Kevin. You prayed for him. You didn't have to be his best friend. You shouldn't feel all this guilt."

He peered into her face and pointed to his chest. "God placed me in his life. I should have been a better witness. If I had been more patient, maybe he would have accepted Christ."

Zoey furrowed her brow. "So now you're God?" She crossed her arms. "That's an awfully arrogant statement, Mark."

Mark blinked and shook his head. He motioned toward the grave site. "A man I should have treated better is dead."

He pointed to himself again. "I'm saying with my mouth, and feeling with my heart, that I should have been a better witness to him." He squinted at her. "And that makes me arrogant? Explain how."

Zoey reached up and touched his cheek. Tenderness shone from her dark eyes. "No. Your believing you were in control of Kevin's choices makes your thinking arrogant. Each person has to choose Christ individually."

"But I should have been a better witness."

"Mark, we all sin and fall short of the glory of God. That means Christians, too."

Zoey's teeth chattered the last few words. Though he couldn't feel anything, he knew it was cold and they'd been standing outside a long time. He put his arm around her and guided her toward the car. In his mind, he knew she was right. But the thought of a man dying lost, without having accepted Christ—Mark shuddered. He'd spend the rest of his life telling everyone he knew about Jesus.

thirteen

Zoey walked into her favorite nail salon. Greeting her technician, she sat down and allowed Kim to start filing down her much-too-long nails. "Do you want a design today?" Kim asked.

Zoey grinned. "You know I do." She pointed to the fourth flower design on the pallet. "I want this one, only just on my ring fingers."

"Okay." Kim went back to work, applying the acrylic then filing the thickness and the tips of the nails until they were the length and shape Zoey wanted. Having spent most of her growing-up years biting her nails down to the nub, Zoey was always thrilled to see her nails neatly manicured and sporting a cool design. She looked at the painted white flower with streaks of pink through the petals and the hot pink gem on both her ring fingers. "Kim, I think this is my favorite design yet."

Kim smiled and pulled a nail tip out of the drawer behind her station. "I'm working on another design."

Zoey oohed over the yellow, pink, and orange lines that framed the edges of the nail. "I may have to try that next time."

Once finished, Zoey pulled the gift certificate Mark had given her as a late Christmas gift from her purse. At first, she had been furious with him for suggesting she needed to curb her spending, but once she admitted to herself, her sister, and Mark that he was right, she'd been striving diligently to live within her means. *And this gift allowed me to pay more than the minimum due on my credit card bill this month.*

She smiled at how good it felt to pay down her bills instead of adding to them. Mark had offered to assist her in writing up a budget, but with the holidays and Kevin's death, they'd never gotten around to it. *I think I'm doing pretty well though. I've cut up all the department store cards I had and kept only one major card for emergencies. And it's frozen in a cube of ice in the freezer.*

Waving good-bye to Kim, Zoey walked out of the shop and into the mall area. The windows of one of her favorite department stores were plastered with post-holiday sale signs. The urge to stop by for a quick look niggled at her gut. She thought of how that particular store allowed its customers to purchase even without the credit card on hand; she simply had to punch her social security number into the machine. *I have to stay strong. There is nothing I need in there.*

She turned her head and walked toward the mall's exit. *What I do need is to find a nail salon that's not in the center of the mall.*

She raised her eyebrows at the thought. It wasn't such a bad idea. It would keep her from being so tempted. As she pondered the possibility, she realized a lot of her shopping sprees happened right after trips to get her nails done.

She really liked Kim, but if the temptation was too great, she was willing to find another place. *Or I could just stop getting my nails done.* She looked down at her pink and white tips and the small white flowers painted on her ring fingernails. *Nah. As long as I can fit it in the budget, I love getting my nails done.*

Tightening her coat around her, she headed to her car. *What I should do is just cancel those cards; then I won't have an account in the stores' systems when I go to get my nails done.* Pleased with the idea, she slipped inside her car and drove toward the bank. She was meeting Mark for lunch. Afterward, she had an interview at the hospital. She wouldn't be able to start in an official dietician position until she graduated in four months, but she could work as a dietary aide. The opportunity to spend a few months getting to know the environment of her job thrilled her, and she prayed the interview would go well.

She pulled into the bank's parking lot and picked up the small paperweight she'd found at the bookstore. There was nothing fancy about it, just brown with black letters engraved on it. But Mark had struggled the last few days since Kevin's funeral, and she knew he needed the message on it: "My peace I give you."

The fact that she'd purchased it for 50 percent off and with the miscellaneous cash she'd allowed herself for this pay period made the gift even better. She hadn't felt the freedom of not purchasing every small item she wanted in a long time. And she loved it.

She pushed open the bank's front door as an older lady was walking out of an office on her left. The woman smiled. "You must be Zoey."

Taken aback, Zoey frowned. "I am."

The woman pointed to Zoey's head. "It's that beautiful red hair, dear. Mark loves it." She extended her hand. "I'm Betty Grimes, the bank manager."

Pleasure coursed through her at the thought that Mark had mentioned her to his manager. He'd talked about the kind lady he worked for, and she was thrilled he'd shared their budding relationship with her. Zoey pulled off her mittens and shook Betty's hand. "It's a pleasure to meet you."

She pointed toward a door on her right. "Mark's in his office. I know he'll be glad to see you."

Zoey could see through the glass walls that he didn't have

a customer with him. His back was turned and he hadn't seen her yet, so she slowly pushed the door all the way open. "Hey, Mark."

He turned to face her. His eyebrows rose and his lips bowed into one of the biggest smiles she'd seen. "I'm glad you're here." He stood and walked to her, embracing her in a teddy bear hug. Her feelings for him seemed to be growing faster than in any other relationship she'd had, and yet he still hadn't kissed her. With each hug, each handhold, she longed for him to touch his lips to hers. *It hasn't been that long. We've only known each other a few months, only considered officially dating a week ago.*

But it seemed longer to her. She already felt connected with him, already felt confirmed that he was God's choice for her. She'd done the "dating thing" all wrong in the past, following her will and wants instead of God's plan for her. Now she didn't want to play games. She was nearing graduation, about to get a job in her field, and she wanted to settle down with the right man. With Mark.

Whoa, that's some heavy thinking, she inwardly chastised herself. *Don't shift the impulsivity from shopping to marriage.* The thought caused Zoey to pause. She'd never realized how quick she was to grab at things, but it was as true as God's Word. Taking a deep breath, she allowed herself to enjoy Mark's hug.

She released him and pulled her small gift from her coat pocket. "I got you a little something."

He raised his eyebrows.

"With cash."

He laughed and took the gift from her hand.

"It's just a little reminder that God wants you to have peace." She took it back from him and set it on a stack of papers. "It's a paperweight."

"Thanks, Zoey." He grabbed her arms. "Let me introduce you to Betty."

"We've already met. She likes my hair."

A blush traipsed up his neck and along his jaw. Deciding to goad him a bit, she grinned. "She mentioned you like it, too."

He reached up and twirled a small strand that had fallen at her shoulder between his fingers. "I really do like it."

The intensity of those chocolate brown eyes was back, and again she wished the man would just lean down and kiss her already. She could make the first move. *But I don't want to; I want him to do it.*

Trying not to let out a long sigh or pass out under his gaze, Zoey fought to read what he was thinking. He bit the bottom of his lip when his gaze moved from her eyes to her mouth. *He's going to do it.*

She closed her eyes, awaiting his touch. Instead, she felt a gentle pressure at her forehead. She opened her eyes to see he'd turned away from her. He picked his keys up off the desk. "Are you ready?"

Warmth flooded Zoey's cheeks. She'd practically thrown her kiss at him and he didn't take it. Exasperated, she shoved her hands in her coat pockets and pulled out her mittens. "Sure. Let's go."

❧

Mark watched Zoey as she shoved a forkful of salad into her mouth. He'd come so close to kissing her. He believed she'd wanted him to as well. But he didn't want to move too fast, didn't want to mess up.

He felt weak since Kevin's death. Raw and tender. God was drawing him closer, and Mark had spent more time in scripture over the last few days than he had in months. Physically, he longed to hold Zoey, to claim her lips against his, but his mind knew he'd gone too far in the past, and though it had been years, he didn't want to make the same mistake with Zoey.

At some point he would tell her what he was like before he accepted Christ into his life. He had been every bit as cocky as Kevin, maybe more so. It was the reason Mark prayed for the man daily and also why he had gotten so angry with his colleague. Mark read Kevin's actions and knew his intentions like he read the label of a cereal box and knew what was inside.

Guilt tried to wend its way back into Mark's heart. *My peace I give you.* The words on the paperweight Zoey had given him slipped into his mind. He breathed the meaning into his heart, allowing it to set up in his mind. *God, You want me to have peace about Kevin. I wasn't a perfect witness, wasn't even a good witness sometimes. But I wanted to be.*

He thought of the scripture where Paul admitted struggling with doing what he didn't want to do and not doing what he should do. The first time Mark had read it, he'd scratched his head in confusion. Now he understood Paul's inner dilemma to the depths of his being.

Mark focused on Zoey. She looked professional and yet so pretty in her dark navy skirt and jacket and baby blue silk blouse. A single strand of pearls hung from her neck, and two small pearls dropped from gold spheres in her ear lobes. Her long red hair was pulled up on the sides with a matching clip. Light pink lipstick covered her lips, making him yearn once again to claim them against his own. "Have I mentioned that you look beautiful?"

"No." Zoey took a sip of her drink. "But I needed to hear that. Thanks."

"Nervous?"

"Very." She traced her fingers along the side of the plate.

"I've wanted a job like this since I decided my major a couple of years ago."

"You want to pray about it?"

She nodded. "I would love that. I can't believe I didn't think of it before. The Bible tells us when two or more are gathered, He hears and answers our prayers."

She reached across the table and grabbed his hand. He twisted it around so that he could caress her palm with his thumb. Her hand was soft and felt perfect in his grasp.

He bowed his head, thanking God for Zoey and her faith in Him and her desire to be in His will. "Calm her nerves, Lord," he prayed. "Guide her through the interview, and if this is the place You have for her to work, may she find favor in the eyes of her interviewers."

He hesitated, feeling the Spirit's nudging to pray for them as a couple. For a moment he worried he would chase her off with the prayer, but his desire to stay in line with God's guidance took over and he continued, "Lord, in the past I've prayed for the woman You have for me. . . ."

He heard Zoey suck in her breath, and she wrapped her hands around his thumbs. He went on, "I care a lot about Zoey. I know You've placed her in my life. May You guide our relationship. May we follow Your lead. Amen."

Mark lifted his head and peeked up at Zoey. She stared at him with just a hint of tears pooling in her eyes. "Thanks, Mark."

❧

As Zoey waited for her interview to begin, she mulled Mark's prayer over in her mind. He was waiting to kiss her. She could hear it in his tone when he prayed and see it in his eyes once he'd finished. She decided she was okay with that. In fact, she felt respected and lifted up by his desire to put God first in their relationship. It was something she believed. A man and woman could know true, complete unity only with God as the center, but to hear the man she was falling for say it aloud—well, it nearly took her breath away and made her fall a little deeper for him.

Trying to focus on the interview, she looked around the small human resources office. Though clean and orderly, the rust- and blue-colored furnishings and light taupe walls were in desperate need of updating. The position she sought was with the oldest hospital in the Wilmington area, which didn't bother her at all. The furnishings may have been a bit on the ancient side, but the patient care was known throughout the city.

Her heartbeat quickened at the thought of working one-on-one with a young mother concerning her child's diet or with an older man who'd been recently diagnosed with a medical condition. She yearned to help others with their nutritional needs. Sometimes the smallest change in diet made the biggest difference in a person's physical well-being.

The director's office door opened and a small, balding, sixtyish man stepped out. "Are you Zoey Coyle?"

His voice sounded very much like Mickey Mouse's; he even crinkled his nose when he spoke. Zoey had to take deep breaths so that a nervous giggle wouldn't slip out. "I am."

"Come in."

He motioned her inside, and she stood and followed him into the room. A tall, thin, middle-aged black woman stood and shook her hand. "Hello, I'm Vera Jeffries."

Zoey learned she was the director of food services. She then met a doctor and the administrator of the hospital. They quizzed her with one question after another, but Zoey found herself focusing on the woman who would be her direct authority. The lady's expressions were firm but kind, and Zoey couldn't help but believe the woman would be terrific to work for.

"I have one last question." Ms. Jeffries leaned forward in her seat. "What made you decide to become a dietician?"

Zoey hesitated. How did she explain without telling more than she wanted? Her initial yearning to learn about foods and how they could and should be used to help the body came after Micah was born. Her poor boy struggled each time he ate, pushing his little legs against his belly as he cried out in pain. He'd drink formula and then spit up; then he'd cry; then he'd spit up some more.

It took several weeks of switching formulas, trying them for a few days, then switching again until they finally learned he was not only lactose intolerant, but also allergic to soy. Cam and Sadie had to buy a special formula for her son, and his belly settled down as soon as the other formulas were out of his system. He was the first living proof she'd witnessed of the smallest of dietary changes making the biggest difference in a person's life. Micah went from hurting and crying to resting and cooing.

Not too long after his birth, she'd also had the opportunity to go on a mission trip to South America. The plight of one family in particular would remain etched in her mind for the rest of her life. The day her group arrived, a young woman buried her infant daughter. Bacteria from unclean water and unsanitary conditions had permeated the baby's body until she didn't have the strength to fight back. It had been the most heart-wrenching experience—especially after having just given birth to Micah—that Zoey had ever witnessed. After that, she became a sponsor of that family.

The memory made her shudder. They weren't the only ones living in deprived conditions. When she saw how sick the people were due to bad water and limited food supplies, something in her just clicked and she knew she wanted to help people eat better.

Weighing her words, she looked at Ms. Jeffries then at the other interviewers. "The first time I knew I wanted to work as a dietician was when. . ." She paused. How should she describe Micah without saying he was her son? *God, I won't lie, but I don't feel it's necessary to share everything, either.* She cleared her throat.

"When a baby was born into our family not only lactose intolerant but also allergic to soy. The baby experienced several weeks of pain before his parents and the doctor were able to diagnose what was wrong." She shook away the memory, feeling it more deeply than someone who wasn't intimately connected to Micah. "It was a hard thing to observe."

Ms. Jeffries nodded. "That poor baby. It happens more often than you'd think, and it just takes time to figure out what will work best for their little digestive systems."

Zoey nodded. "Second was when I went on a mission trip."

The woman sat back in her chair. "Tell us about that."

As she began to share, Ms. Jeffries nodded in a way that let Zoey know she knew exactly what Zoey was talking about. She continued to share until the woman finally told them she'd spent ten years with her missionary parents in Africa. It was where she'd developed the desire to go into dietetics. Zoey's heart warmed as she felt a kindred spirit with the woman. When it was time to leave, Ms. Jeffries grabbed her hand. "I'll be in touch soon."

Zoey nodded. *God, I believe You led me to this place.*

fourteen

Mark eyed the chocolate chip cookies one of the customers had dropped off at the bank in celebration of Valentine's Day. It was Friday, his splurge day this week, but he and Zoey were planning to have dinner then stop by his mom's house. Their original board game night had been pushed back a couple of weeks because of Kevin's funeral and because Mark simply hadn't felt up to it. But God had remained faithful during this time, and Mark didn't want to disappoint his mom and sister by not being able to eat the goodies they'd inevitably fix for the occasion.

You don't need one, Mark.

He tried to look away, but it was like the treat had some kind of magnetic draw. His stomach growled for no reason. He knew he wasn't hungry; he'd had lunch only an hour ago. His feet seemed to move of their own accord toward the coffeepot and the counter that held the homemade goodies.

I'm like an addict drawn to my drug. I'm not even hungry, but I want one so bad.

He forced himself to look away. He thought of the fight he and Zoey had weeks ago when he confronted her about her excessive credit card use and she accused him of splurging a little more than he should.

And she was right, God. Mark urged his feet toward the restroom. He peered at his reflection in the mirror above the sink. *I've lost thirty-five pounds. My blood pressure is under control, and Dr. Carr is thinking of taking me off medication on a trial basis.*

Though they weren't dirty, he washed and dried his hands. The image of the plate of cookies popped into his mind. Knowing who baked them made the temptation even worse, because she made the best cookies in the world. *This is ridiculous. What's one cookie going to hurt?*

He rushed out of the bathroom and toward the counter. His cell phone vibrated in his pocket. He pulled it out. *Zoey.* He grinned as he flipped open the phone. "Hey."

"Hi. How's your day going?"

"Trying to keep myself from devouring a plate of home-made cookies."

"Don't do it." Zoey's voice sounded urgent. "Splurge night is tonight, and you've been doing so good. Think about it. I haven't spent any money on credit cards, and you haven't cheated with foods."

Mark laughed as he pivoted and walked away from the cookies and back toward his office. "I think God encouraged you to call right now."

"Probably so." Zoey popped her tongue. "Guess what else God did?"

Mark plopped down in his leather chair and leaned as far back as it would allow. "I don't know. What?"

"Got me that job at the hospital."

Mark leaned forward and smacked the top of his desk. "Zoey, that's wonderful. You had a feeling you'd get it."

"I really did." She must have opened the door because he heard the dinging of her car. "I'm heading into the gym. I'll see you later. No cookies."

Though she couldn't see him, he saluted the phone. "You got it." Shoving it back in his pocket, he turned toward his computer and started working on a loan he needed to finish before he left for the day.

God, I think You did have Zoey call me at that exact moment.

He looked up at the ceiling, marveling that God was involved in the small and big things of his life. *Thanks.*

⁊⛟

Zoey could hardly wait to visit Mark's mom and sister. The one time she'd met them, she could tell they'd be a lot of fun to be around. There was also no guessing what they'd tell her about Mark, and she thought that would be pretty funny, too.

Mark stopped in front of his mom's front door and waved his arms in front of her. "Whatever they say—"

Zoey laughed. "It will be fine."

Mark smacked his hands against his thighs. "Yeah. It will be fine for you. There's no telling what they'll say about me."

She shuffled her eyebrows. "I can't wait to know all your dark, sordid secrets."

Mark shook his head and rolled his eyes as he unlocked his mom's door then pushed it open. "Mom, we're here."

Before Zoey could fully step through the door, she was attacked by a younger, female version of Mark. The woman yanked off Zoey's mittens while an older woman pulled off her coat. "We're so glad you could come," his mom said.

"We're going to have the best time," Maddy added. "Mom and I have put every game we own out on the table. Tonight you get to pick." She clapped her hands together, a motion that took Zoey's thoughts back to seventh grade.

Zoey smiled, knowing the night would be carefree and entertaining. "Terrific. You all wouldn't happen to have Scattergories?"

"She's a word-game girl." Mark's mom, Sylvia, patted Maddy's forearm.

"We have it," Maddy answered.

"Oh no," Mark whined. "Not another woman to kick my behind at word games."

Zoey giggled as she followed Sylvia and Maddy to the

dining area. Games of every size and shape were piled on one side, while several plates of veggies, fruits, sandwiches, crackers, and dips covered the other side. Zoey pointed at the food. "The food looks delicious. I won't have to eat for a week."

"Wait until you try Mom's homemade cheese dip." Mark grabbed a cracker, scooped a helping of the creamy cheese onto it, then popped it in his mouth. "Mmm. This is why I'm glad I skipped the cookies."

Sylvia moved the games onto the floor then set up Scattergories while Maddy, Mark, and Zoey filled their plates with snacks. "How many pounds have you lost, son?"

"The last time I weighed, it was thirty-five pounds. My goal is forty, and my last weigh-in is a month from Monday. For the bank competition, anyway."

"You look great, big brother." Maddy smacked at Mark's belly. "Feel them tight abs."

Mark pushed her away. "Don't feel them too hard, or I'll throw up on you."

Zoey chuckled as she sat down in one of the four chairs around the square table. She looked around the room. Most of the furnishings were older, but the house was clean and smelled like freshly baked brownies. Tonight would definitely be splurge night.

She grabbed a pen from the stack in the center of the table and doodled on the notepad to be sure it had ink in it. Maddy sat across from her. She tapped her pen against the wood. "So you're graduating this year?"

"Yeah. I just found out I got a job at the hospital where I applied, too."

Sylvia sat on her left. "That's great."

"That is exciting!" Maddy exclaimed. "What kind of job?"

"I'm going to be a dietician."

Mark added, "And she's going to be a great one." He pointed at his belly. "Look what a super job she's done on me."

Maddy rolled her eyes then winked at Zoey. "But he's not yet strong enough to take a little tummy tap from his baby sister."

"Tummy tap?" he bellowed. "You almost made me hurl all over the place. I hope you don't tummy tap Bruce like that."

Maddy crinkled her nose. "Bruce?"

"Bruce?" His mother added and gawked at Maddy.

Maddy shook her head. "Bruce and I are just friends." She looked at her mother. "I mean it. We really are."

Mark frowned. "Really? But I thought. . ."

Noting the tension that was quickly thickening in the room, Zoey chuckled and changed the subject. "Mark's been doing a good job. No cheating for a while now."

Mark's demeanor loosened, and he looked at Maddy and stuck out his tongue. She did the same.

"Would you two stop it?" Sylvia swatted at both of them.

Maddy raked her fingers through her long, sandy-colored hair then tied it up in a ponytail with the band she had around her wrist. Her small, fair features and bubbly personality made her seem years younger than Zoey. "I'm a year behind due to the leukemia. But you know," Maddy continued, "I wouldn't change it. I learned so much about my faith and about myself during that time."

She glanced at Mark, and Zoey knew that though she looked young, she'd physically experienced more than most people twice her age. With that experience came wisdom.

"I've learned to enjoy each moment. To be honest and up front." Maddy smiled and shrugged her shoulders as she turned her attention back toward Zoey. "To just be who I am."

"I'll toast to that." Sylvia lifted her soft drink toward the center of the table. Zoey laughed as she lifted hers and clinked cans with Mark's mom then Maddy.

When she reached for Mark's can, his gaze captured hers. He mouthed, "I need to talk to you later."

She nodded then placed her drink back on the table. Maddy's words weighed on Zoey's heart. She still hadn't told Mark about Micah. It wasn't fair to keep such a thing from the person she was falling in love with. *What if he already knows about Micah? What if he figured it out when I was showing him those pictures? Maybe he wants to talk to me because I haven't told him the full truth about myself.*

She tried to focus on the game when Sylvia rolled the letter dice and started the timer. Normally she was an excellent word-game player. But she couldn't stop thinking of how she should have been honest with Mark a week or more ago. Game after game she lost to Sylvia, then Maddy, then Maddy again, then Sylvia.

After a couple of hours, Mark threw down his notepad. "Ladies, I think you've beat me enough tonight."

Zoey scrunched her nose. "Me, too." She dropped her pen on the table. "I used to do better than that."

Reaching across the table, Maddy high-fived her mom. "Or maybe Mom and I are just that good."

Zoey lifted her index finger in the air. "Touché. You and Sylvia are definitely good."

Mark stood up and piled the women's plates on top of his. "I'll get the dishes."

Sylvia gingerly set a mug on top of his pile. "You're frootin' tootin' you will."

Zoey lifted her eyebrows, and Maddy leaned across the table. "It's the only slang term my mom uses. We have no idea where she came up with it. It's like a cross between the sound of a train and a bowl of Froot Loops."

Zoey laughed out loud, and Mark shook his head and

motioned for her to join him in the kitchen. She picked up the empty soda cans. "I'll help Mark."

"Okay," Sylvia said. "We'll put away the games."

Zoey rinsed the cans then tossed them into the recycling bin while Mark rinsed off the dishes. She pulled a dishrag off a cabinet handle. "Your mom and sister are hilarious."

"Just a barrel of laughs."

"No, I mean it."

Mark turned off the water and wiped his hands on a towel. "Maddy did touch on something that I want to talk to you about." Mark folded his arms in front of his chest and leaned against the counter. "I want to kiss you, Zoey."

Warmth filled Zoey's cheeks, and her heart sped up. *Finally! God, I'm so ready for him to just kiss me already.*

"But I'm not going to."

The excitement streaming through her heart plunged to her feet and right out of her manicured toenails. "Okay."

"Not yet anyway." He turned away from her then looked up at the ceiling. "The truth is, I didn't know Christ in high school. I was a highly sought-after quarterback with a big ego, and I didn't always treat girls as I should have."

Zoey watched as Mark wrung his hands together. She reached for his hand. "Mark, we've all made mistakes."

He shook his head and pulled away. "No. I mean, yes, but..." He turned to face her. "Zoey, the things that made me sick about Kevin were just as true about me. I used girls for my own satisfaction and nothing else. I didn't care how they felt or what they wanted, just how they made me feel. That's why I couldn't stand for Kevin to be around you. I knew what he was thinking, what he wanted to do."

Surprised, Zoey sucked in the forwardness of his confession. Sudden jealousy slithered through her as she wondered about his high school years. Then her own mistakes flashed to the front of her mind. She needed to tell him about Micah, to let him know that she had made bad choices, that she had been selfish, only thinking of herself. That she had needed God's forgiveness and mercy just as much as he had. "Mark—"

"Listen." He captured a lock of her hair between his fingers. "When I became a Christian, I vowed never to act like that again, and I haven't. Then I met you, and you've set my emotions to spinning." He bent down and gently kissed the strand of hair. "And I won't disrespect you like that. I care about you. A lot."

Love filled her heart for the overgrown man. If he asked her to marry him that instant, she'd pack her bags and head to the church. But she had to be honest with him as well. "Mark, I need to tell you something."

He moved closer to her. "What?"

She gazed into his deep chocolate eyes. The love he felt for her was evident in those dark pools. She didn't want to do or say anything to hurt him or to make him care for her less. *Dear Jesus, help me be honest.*

Irrational fear raced through her, and a vision of Micah's dad running off when she told him she was pregnant passed through her mind. She didn't want to lose Mark. *But I have to tell him.*

"Mark, I . . ."

The words wouldn't come. They stuck to the back of her throat.

"What?"

She looked at him, mentally begging him not to run off as Micah's dad had. She blew out a breath. She couldn't say it. Not now. "Would you be willing to visit my parents next weekend?"

His face brightened, and he kissed her forehead. "Absolutely."

fifteen

Mark walked into the bank. He shrugged out of his coat and hung it on the rack. Though spring officially started in a week, April and May would pass before Wilmington warmed up to his liking. Twenty weeks. Their officewide competition had been going on for twenty weeks. At times it felt much longer, and yet the time had flown by. Anxious to find out the results of the "biggest loser" contest, he was the first in the office. He made his way to the counter, pulled out a coffee filter and coffee, and started the brew. *It doesn't matter to me if I win; I just want to know if I lost forty pounds.*

He walked back to the conference room. Someone had left the light on. He flicked off the light and a squeal and commotion sounded from inside the room.

What in the world? He turned the light back on and walked inside. His manager sat on the floor covered in balloons. "Betty? Are you all right? I didn't know you were in here."

"I'm okay." Betty laughed as she stood to her feet and placed a pair of scissors on the table. "I'm just glad I didn't stab myself." She pointed to the split bag tied to the ceiling light. "I figured we'd pull the string and drop a bunch of balloons on the winner. I was trying to make the string a bit shorter when you turned out the lights. I stabbed the bag, and the balloons and I went tumbling down."

A vision of Betty plunging the knife in her stomach popped into his mind and he shook away the horrible image. "I didn't think anyone was here. I didn't see your car outside."

"It's broken down. My husband had to drop me off this

146

morning." She motioned toward the door. "Now go get me another trash bag from under the coffeepot and help me get these balloons in it. Remember, we weigh in at eight o'clock sharp."

Mark looked at his watch. It was 7:30. They didn't have much time to fill a bag with balloons and tie it to the ceiling as well as get the bank ready to be opened, but Betty had been so excited about the contest that Mark didn't have the heart to disappoint her.

Together they shoved the balloons into the bag. She tied it while he attached it to the light so that the string could be pulled and the balloons would fall. With only a few minutes before business hours, they raced around getting computers, money, and other office equipment ready for the day.

He watched Betty happily scramble around the bank. She was as excited as he had ever seen her. Though he still wanted to make his goal, he sincerely hoped Betty was the overall victor.

Within moments the office buzzed with workers, ten of whom were participating in the competition. Betty clapped her hands. "Are we ready for weigh-in?"

"We sure are," the night custodian said. Mark noticed he'd lost a good amount of weight as well.

Barb called them up one at a time. Because several of the employees didn't want their actual weight told to the entire office, Barb wrote down their weight then used a calculator to figure out who'd lost the greatest percentage.

After several long, agonizing minutes, she lifted a piece of paper in her hand. "I have the results right here." Grinning from ear to ear, she pointed at each one who had participated. "One of you will take home this lovely treadmill." She motioned to the already-assembled machine that had been donated by a local department store.

Betty twisted in her spot. "Oh Barb, hurry up already."

Barb took a deep breath. "Okay, the winner is. . ." She pointed to the piece of paper. "And by the way, this person lost ten pounds more than his or her goal. I have been so proud of this person and his or her efforts to not only win the prize, but also get back into shape. I—"

"Barb," Betty whined.

The woman huffed then turned an exaggerated smile toward Mark's office manager. "The winner is Betty Grimes."

Betty's face lit up like Maddy's had when their dad purchased her first cell phone. Excitement for his manager welled within him. She'd worked hard and had wanted to win so badly. Mark waited until she stood next to Barb; he pulled the string, allowing the balloons to fall on top of her for the second time that morning.

He walked to her and wrapped her in a hug. "I'm so happy for you, Betty."

"I can't believe it, Mark." She pressed her palm against her cheek. "And I feel so much better with less weight. What was your final total?"

"I'm getting ready to find out." Mark turned to Barb. "What was my final weight?"

She flipped through the cards until she reached his. "Two hundred thirty-seven."

"Two hundred thirty-seven?"

Barb smiled and nudged him with her elbow. "Good job, Mark."

Two hundred thirty-seven! His goal had been two hundred forty. He'd lost a total of forty-three pounds. *Thank You, Jesus.* He pulled his phone out of his front pocket. He couldn't wait to tell Zoey.

❧

Zoey followed her sister into the church's gymnasium. She'd

never attended this particular church, and she was over-whelmed at the size of it. Brittany walked past the basketball court, up the stairs, and past several classrooms until she finally stopped in front of a door. Brittany pushed a lock of hair behind her ear. "I'm really glad you agreed to come with me tonight."

"Of course. Why wouldn't I?"

"Well, I kind of have an ulterior motive." Brittany pulled the lock back out from behind her ear and shoved it into her mouth.

Zoey put her hands on her hips, recognizing her sister's nervous gesture. "Brittany. What are you up to?"

"Well. . ." Brittany pulled the hair out of her mouth and twirled it between her fingers. "There's this guy."

Zoey's mouth dropped. "You're kidding me."

Brittany dropped the hair and lifted both palms toward Zoey. "Listen. This guy is a Christian. It's obvious. You'll be able to tell right away. And, well. . ." She bounced on the balls of her feet.

"Well?"

"Well, I think he's going to ask me out, and I'm nervous about it, and I don't know what to say, and if he does, I want you to be with me." Brittany blew the words out in one breath.

Overwhelmed with thanksgiving, Zoey wrapped her arms around her sister. The Brittany she knew—the carefree, funny, even dramatic sister she'd grown up with—was returning. Zoey had feared Neil had squelched her sister's sweet spirit. *Why did I fear, Lord? You are greater than Neil Thurman.* "Of course I'll be here for you. Do you need me to get out my sister radar?"

Brittany laughed. "I'm telling you, Zoey, you'll like this one."

"Okay, then lead the way."

Brittany pushed her hair behind her shoulders then flattened the bright pink button-down shirt against her jeans. Whoever the mystery guy was, Zoey had no doubt that he had noticed her tall and beautiful sister.

Brittany opened the door. The chairs were set up in a semicircle. Zoey followed Brittany to two empty ones. As they sat down, Zoey scanned the room for possible beaus for Brittany. Several guys were sitting around the circle, but all of them seemed to be with a girl. A few minutes passed and more college students walked in, but she still couldn't pick out anyone whom Brittany might be interested in dating.

She leaned toward her sister. "Maybe he's not coming."

"He'll be here."

Zoey looked at her watch. It was almost time to start. The leader would be walking in at any minute. The door opened and a tall, thin man walked inside. He looked familiar, as if she knew him from somewhere, but Zoey couldn't quite put her finger on it. He looked at Zoey and recognition passed across his features. He pointed at her. "Zoey Coyle?"

She pursed her lips. "I know I know you, but I just can't place—"

He pointed to himself. "Logan Huff. I was in your mom's senior English class with you—for a while anyway." He grabbed her hand and shook it. "How are you doing? How's your mom?"

"Great. I'm great. She's great." She pointed to her little sister, who stood a good five inches taller than Zoey. "Did you know she was my sister?"

Logan glanced at Brittany. Crimson budded on his cheeks, but he didn't take his eyes from her. "Brittany, I didn't realize Ms. Coyle—I mean, Ms. Smith—was your mom."

Brittany clasped her hands together and rocked back on her heels. "Well, she was both that year, huh?"

Zoey tried to place Logan. Her senior year had been crazy with her mom getting married, then Zoey finding out she was pregnant and deciding to finish the year as a home schooler. A memory of a tall, gangly guy who liked to hang around his mom's desk, talking to her all the time, paraded into her mind.

She snapped her fingers. "I remember you. You led the prayer group at school." She frowned. It was funny how she just suddenly remembered that. Her mom had encouraged her repeatedly to try it out, constantly telling her what a nice guy Logan Huff was.

"Yes, I did. I'll be graduating this May; then I'm going to start at seminary in the fall."

Zoey smiled. "That's wonderful. I graduate this May, too. I'm going to be a dietician. In fact, I just got a job."

"Good for you." Logan looked at the clock on the wall, then back at Zoey and Brittany. His gaze seemed to linger a bit longer on Brittany, and Zoey's heart warmed at the idea of he and Brittany getting to know each other better. She knew her mom would be thrilled, too.

"We've got to get started, but would you two like to go for a coffee after the study"—he gazed at Brittany again—"to catch up?"

Zoey's heart nearly burst with excitement for her sister. "I think we'd love that."

Both of them sat down, and Brittany leaned close to Zoey. Her voice was giddy as she whispered, "I told you you would like him."

sixteen

Mark peered out the windshield. He couldn't help but enjoy the serenity of the nature around him. He reached over and took Zoey's hand in his. She seemed more nervous than he did about his meeting her family. If her family was as crazy as his, he understood her concern. He squeezed her hand. "You know I'm going to love your family."

"Mmm-hmm."

Focusing on his surroundings, he noticed the land looked like snow-covered ocean waves, rolling high and low on each side. Large bare trees covered much of the ground without cluttering it. Occasionally they passed a large pond. Though frozen, the water brought back vivid memories of fishing with his dad.

Zoey pointed ahead. "There's Cam and Sadie's house." Mark spotted a stone house with a room built onto the side. The exterior walls of the room were made of nothing but windows. Several bushes and small trees lined the front of the house. He could imagine how beautiful the place looked in the spring when everything budded to life.

"You've got to be a little nervous." Zoey's voice was little more than a whisper, and her gaze stayed focused on the house ahead.

"A little, but not really. I'm excited to meet your family."

He'd known Zoey almost five months. They'd been dating for only two, but already Mark felt confident she was the woman he'd ask to be his wife. So many people he knew dated for a year or more before they got engaged, and normally he thought that was a good idea. But with Zoey, he was ready.

He pulled into the driveway, glancing at Zoey as he took the keys from the ignition. Her face had paled several shades. He couldn't imagine why she was so anxious about his meeting her family.

"Mom and Harold aren't here yet."

"That's okay. You can introduce me to your aunt and uncle, and don't you have a couple of cousins?"

She nodded, never looking at him. "Ellie and. . .Micah."

Mark snapped his fingers. "Yeah. He's the one with red hair like yours."

Zoey nodded. She clasped and unclasped her hands then picked at the skin on the side of her thumb. "I need to tell you something. I was going to tell you later, but maybe now is as good a time as any—"

"Zoey!" A small red-haired boy opened the front door and traipsed down the steps as fast as his little feet would take him. He didn't have a coat on.

A dark-haired woman raced out the front door behind him. "Micah, get back in here. Zoey will be in the house in just a minute."

Zoey swung open the door and scooped the boy in her arms before the dark-haired woman could catch him. "Hey, my little man."

Zoey kissed Micah's nose and cuddled him close to her. The resemblance between the cousins was uncanny. She tickled his chin and the little guy laughed, showing deep dimples in his cheeks, just like Zoey's.

"Let's get you inside, Micah." Zoey motioned for Mark to follow her.

He stepped out of the car and the dark-haired woman shook his hand. "Hi. I'm Sadie. It's a pleasure to meet you."

"Mark. I'm happy to meet you, too."

He followed Zoey's aunt into the house and was introduced to her uncle Cam and cousin Ellie. "Sadie, your daughter looks just like you." He walked to Zoey, who still held Micah, and rubbed the boy's hair. "So where'd you get your hair, little guy?"

Ellie laughed. "From Zoey, of course."

The room grew silent, and Mark watched as Cam, Sadie, and Zoey looked hesitantly at one another.

Ellie scratched her head then turned toward her mother. "I'm going to go put my special babies up before Rachel and Rebecca get here."

Cam chuckled. "Good idea."

Mark looked at Zoey and lifted his eyebrows. "Your little sisters, right?"

Zoey nodded. "God blessed Mom and Harold with beautiful little rascals."

Mark studied Zoey and Micah. She cared for this little cousin. A lot. Her attention almost never diverted to Ellie. Not that Zoey was unkind to the girl, but she simply didn't put Micah down. He seemed every bit as smitten with her. She held him tight as she plopped onto the couch. Mark sat beside her and Micah. "Was there something you were going to tell me, Zoey?"

She patted Micah's hair back and kissed his forehead. "Yes. As you can see, I'm pretty close to Micah—"

"We're here!" The front door slammed open and a small blond child walked into the room. A matching girl followed, only her hair seemed crooked on one side.

A frazzled yet attractive older version of Zoey, only with darker hair, walked behind the girls carrying a plate covered with aluminum foil. "Rachel, use your inside voice."

A large, gray-haired man followed behind her holding two more dishes, and another girl, this one a teenager, followed behind him.

Zoey sighed when she looked back at Mark. "That's my family."

A loud guffaw echoed through the room as Zoey's uncle Cam rubbed the head of the child whose hair was crooked. He looked at Harold. "Rachel get ahold of the scissors?"

Zoey's mom groaned. "Yes. Just before we left." She turned toward Mark and Zoey. "You must be Mark."

Mark stood and shook hands with Zoey's mother, Kelly, her stepfather, Harold, and her younger sister Candy. He tried to talk to the twin girls, but they didn't stay in one place long enough.

Her mother frowned. "Didn't Brittany come with you?"

Mark watched as Zoey's face lit up. She smiled so big he thought her dimples would disappear inside her cheeks. "She's coming on her own." Zoey rolled back on her heels. "With a date."

"It better not be Neil." Her stepfather folded his arms in front of his chest. The man was every bit as big as Mark, and Mark believed if he were Neil, he wouldn't want to mess with him. Linebacker for Wilmington or not. "I'll not have that boy step foot—"

"I agree," Cam added.

Zoey shook her head. "No, it's not Neil. It's a surprise."

Mark looked at Zoey. She hadn't told him that Brittany was dating someone. He was glad to hear it wasn't Neil. He also noticed Zoey still hadn't put Micah down. She'd hugged her mom, her stepdad, and all her sisters with Micah planted firmly on her hip.

"Surprise!"

Mark looked toward the door as yet another person headed inside the house. He wasn't used to this much family. Even when they visited his mom's siblings for a Christmas celebration, there were fewer people.

Her mom covered her mouth then spread her arms wide. "Logan Huff, I haven't seen you in years." She wrapped her arms around the tall, thin guy.

When Brittany followed behind, Mark realized this guy must be her date, and he must have been someone already approved by the family.

Zoey grabbed his shirt and pulled him close to her. "We still need to talk. After dinner, okay?"

Mark nodded. He had a feeling he knew what she was going to say.

&

"You still haven't told him about Micah?"

Zoey stopped cutting the chocolate cake Sadie had made for dessert and looked at Brittany. "I haven't." She placed the knife on the counter and licked her fingertips. "It's not like I haven't tried. It seems like one thing or another happens and I don't get to tell him."

"If your feelings are as strong as I think they are," her mom said as she took small plates out of the cabinet and placed them on the counter, "then you need to tell him."

"I know it's scary." Sadie took the milk out of the refrigerator, shut the door, then put her arm around Zoey's shoulder and said, "But you gotta do it."

Tears swelled in Zoey's eyes. "What if he runs?"

Kelly huffed. "He won't run."

"Jamie did." For weeks, since she'd realized how much she cared for Mark, Zoey had been haunted by the expression on Micah's biological dad's face when she told him she was pregnant. As if it happened yesterday, she could still see him turn around and walk away.

"Micah is part of who you are." Sadie cupped Zoey's chin with her thumb and finger and stared into her eyes. "I know you wouldn't change that."

"Not even for a minute."

"Then go." Sadie released her chin and pointed toward the living room where Mark, Cam, Logan, and Harold were watching a basketball game.

Brittany giggled when a buzzer sounded from the television. "See, it's even halftime."

Kelly handed her two plates of chocolate cake. "And here's some dessert. You're all set."

"I think I'll wait on the dessert, Mom. But thanks." She exhaled a long breath and flattened her sweater against her jeans. "Okay, I'm going."

Zoey walked into the foyer and grabbed their coats off the rack then walked to the living area. "Hey, Mark, would you care to talk with me a minute?"

Mark's expression seemed so serious when he looked up at her. He smiled, but it was forced, and she feared what he would say when she told him the truth.

She pointed to the back door. "We could sit by the pond. It's frozen, but—"

Cam interrupted her. "Personally, it's my favorite spot."

"Sounds good." Mark took his coat from Zoey's grip and put it on. He opened the back door, allowing her to walk outside first.

They walked the thirty or so steps in silence until they reached her uncle's favorite bench. She sat down and he sat beside her. She watched as he clasped his hands then rubbed them together. "I suppose this is when you're going to tell me Micah is your son."

She sucked in her breath and looked up at him. "You knew?"

He shrugged. "Zoey, a person would have to be blind not to see how much the two of you look alike. And it's obvious he holds a very special place in your heart."

Zoey looked at her hands. She rubbed her finger against the pink gem on the nail tip of her ring finger. "I was scared to tell you. I was so young. So stupid. I didn't know what you would think of me."

"How old were you when you had him?"

"Eighteen. Barely. I got pregnant during my senior year of high school." She peered into Mark's eyes, praying she would still see love in those pools. "I made a lot of mistakes in high school, too. I guess the difference between you and me is that you weren't a Christian. I was. I was just fighting God with everything that was in me."

"Why?"

"My dad's death." She leaned back on the bench and stared at the frozen pond. "I didn't understand why God would take my dad."

"Do you know now?"

"No. I don't." Zoey gazed up at the clear, crisp sky. "But I know God is sovereign, even when I don't understand. I can trust Him."

She laughed as her own words smacked her in the face. She'd been so afraid Mark wouldn't want anything to do with her once he found out about Micah. God already knew how Mark would respond, and whatever happened, He was sovereign.

"What's so funny?"

Zoey looked at the confused expression on Mark's face. "I haven't told you because I've been so scared you'd run. Yet again, I wasn't trusting God."

Mark stared at her for several moments until her heart felt as if it were sinking into her stomach. "Are you gonna run?"

"I admit when we first walked in and I noticed how he clung to you and how you just wouldn't put him down—well, I started to figure that you were more than cousins. In my head I started doing the math."

He shifted his focus to the frozen pond, and Zoey thought her heart would freeze with fear. He looked back at her. "You were very young."

She bit her bottom lip and exhaled slowly. "I was barely out of high school when he was born."

"I'm surprised—and at first, I was a little hurt, confused about why you didn't tell me, taken aback that you've actually carried a baby for nine months—"

"Are you going to run?"

He touched her cheek with the back of his hand. A shiver traveled up her spine at his cold touch. "Why would I run from the woman I love?"

Zoey bit her bottom lip. "You love me?"

"Completely. God has restored both of us." Mark leaned closer to her. He cupped her chin and lifted her face. Before she could respond, Mark gently touched his lips to hers.

Surprised, she drew in a breath. Then he pressed his lips against hers again, this time with more urgency. She ran her fingers through his hair, realizing she'd never enjoyed a kiss more than she did at that moment.

When he finally released her, she blinked several times. "I thought you weren't going to kiss me."

The intensity she yearned to see returned to his deep chocolate eyes. "Zoey Coyle, I'm going to marry you."

"You are?"

"I am." He stood up then grabbed her hand until she stood facing him. "Is that okay with you?"

She nodded. "Uh-huh." She touched his lips with her fingertip. "Would you like to kiss me again?"

Mark laughed. "Once you tell me you love me."

Zoey rose to her tiptoes and threw her arms around his neck, squeezing him as tightly as she could. "I love you."

"That sounds good."

He bent his head down and captured her lips again. Zoey felt as if the heavens applauded and God sat on His throne nodding His approval. She'd prayed for the man God would give her, and He'd sent Mark. *Thank You, Jesus.*

seventeen

Mark peered in the mirror and tried to adjust his boutonniere. He hadn't been convinced about the Independence Day theme when Zoey first mentioned it, but the more she spoke of freedom from debt, freedom from food, and freedom from past mistakes, the more he realized he wanted to begin their marriage acknowledging those things while they freely pledged their lives together before God and their families.

"Are you ready?"

Mark turned at the sound of his sister's voice. His heart ached at her sunken cheeks and frail frame. The red bridesmaid dress hung from her shoulders like it would on a clothes hanger. Not even a week after he'd asked Zoey to marry him, Maddy discovered the cancer had returned. This time with a vengeance.

He made his way to his sister and gently wrapped his arms around her. "You look beautiful, Maddy."

"Thanks, big brother." Tears filled her eyes as she wrapped her bony arms around him. "I praise God He allowed me to see this day."

He fought the knot in the back of his throat as he tried to keep his own tears from falling.

Maddy pulled away from him. "Don't be sad, Mark. Please don't be sad." She adjusted his tie and smoothed the lapels of his tuxedo. "God has a purpose for all things, and I'm ready to see Jesus."

"But we're not ready."

"You have to be. It's His sovereign will."

Mark looked up at the ceiling as he remembered the night Zoey had told him about Micah. She'd fought God all through high school after her father's death, making several bad choices, until she finally accepted that God was sovereign.

He kissed the top of Maddy's head. "I know, sis."

She patted his chest. "Now, we will have no more of this sad stuff. This is the happiest day of your life." She smiled. "And I've seen your bride. She's beautiful."

Mark's heart swelled at the thought of seeing Zoey in her wedding gown. She wouldn't tell him anything about it, except that she'd chosen to wear white. Pure white. As a symbol that God had cleansed her and made her pure again. He couldn't have agreed more. He looked at his watch. "I'd better get out there."

Maddy hugged him one last time. "That's what I came for, to get you."

Mark walked into the sanctuary and stood beside his groomsmen. Logan leaned over and nudged his arm. "Are you ready?"

Mark straightened his jacket. "More ready than I've ever been in my life."

Though he knew it was a matter of minutes before his bride would be walking down the aisle to him, it seemed to take hours. He looked out at the crowd, spying several of his family and friends, as well as several people he'd never seen before in his life. Betty caught his eye and waved. He smiled and waved back at her.

The expectant gazes from the audience started to make him feel queasy, so he focused on the flowers and ribbons that Zoey and her mom, aunt, and sisters had arranged. Red and white were the predominant colors with just a smattering of blue. No one would guess the independence theme unless told. He liked that.

Even more so, he liked the way the white and the red ribbons blended together. It was by Christ's blood that they were made pure and white as snow, and that was the ultimate freedom.

Mark jumped when the music started. His heart raced and his chest tightened. At that moment, God's blessing and mercy overwhelmed him. He couldn't wait to take Zoey's hands and promise to love and cherish her for the rest of his life.

The sanctuary doors opened, and Zoey's cousin and junior bridesmaid, Ellie, walked down the aisle. Mark smiled at her and prayed to be patient as Zoey's sister Candy followed, then his sister, Maddy, then Zoey's aunt Sadie, and finally her maid of honor, Brittany. It felt like the entire city was going to walk down the aisle before his bride.

He sucked in his breath. If he remembered the rehearsal right, Zoey was next. Instead her twin sisters and Micah appeared in the door. Rachel nudged Rebecca, and Rebecca frowned and tried to shove Rachel. Rachel turned around and yelled, "Dad, Rebecca won't go."

Micah shrugged then walked dutifully down the aisle and took his place beside his father.

The audience chuckled as the girls continued to stand at the entrance until Harold appeared. He leaned over and whispered something to both girls. The twins intertwined fingers and stepped into the aisle at the same time. Mark couldn't help but smile as the girls sang, "Left, right, left, right," as they made their way to the front. Once they reached Mark, Rachel turned and hollered, "Dad, do we stop now?"

Mark leaned over. "You did good, girls."

Candy grabbed their hands and pulled them over to the side, and Rachel and Rebecca straightened their shoulders and grinned at the audience.

Mark sneaked a peek at Zoey's mom, Kelly, in the front row. Her hand covered her mouth, and her face blazed crimson.

The wedding march started, and Mark focused on the entrance again. The ushers closed the doors, and when they opened them again, his bride stood there on the arm of her stepdad.

Layers of lace and sparkles hugged her tiny frame to perfection. The mass of material at her feet glistened in the light. A veil covered her face, and Mark could hardly wait for her to reach him so he could peer into her beautiful eyes.

Finally, she stood just feet from him, and it took all his willpower not to grab her into his arms. The pastor spoke, but Mark didn't hear what he said.

Harold's voice boomed, "Her mother and I do." Then Harold lifted her veil and kissed her cheek.

Mark was speechless. Frozen in place. Zoey Coyle was about to become his wife. How he loved this woman. He blinked, and Logan nudged him forward.

He feared his heart would burst from his chest as he took her hand in his. "I love you," he whispered as they moved closer to the pastor.

"I love you, too."

❧

Zoey didn't know how a person could feel more blessed. The man she loved stood beside her, holding her hand, about to vow to spend the rest of his life with her. *God, You are too good to me.*

She looked into his eyes as the pastor asked Mark if he promised to love her, to cherish her, to honor her. The "I do" that slipped from his lips warmed her from the tip of her head to the soles of her feet.

When it was her turn to make the same promise, she prayed he could see to the depth of her soul how much she meant her answer. She loved him completely, but it was more than a feeling. It was a commitment. She looked forward to the opportunity to choose to love Mark day in and day out for the rest of their lives.

The pastor's voice rang out through the sanctuary again. "By the power vested in me and the State of Delaware, I now pronounce you husband and wife. You may kiss your bride."

Zoey's heart raced as Mark placed his hand against her cheek. "I love you, Zoey White."

She relished the sound of his last name alongside her first. "I love you, too."

She closed her eyes as he gently pressed his lips to hers then released her. She opened her eyes and looked at him. A smiled edged its way up her lips. "That's not good enough, Mr. White."

She wrapped her arms around his neck and pulled his lips back to hers. "You're my husband," she mouthed against his lips. "You can really kiss me now."

He chuckled as he squeezed her closer to him, kissing her with a mixture of gentleness and firmness. After several moments, he finally released her.

She blew out a long breath. "You can kiss me like that anytime you'd like, Mr. White."

"You promise?"

Before she could answer affirmatively, he pressed his lips to hers yet again. She'd never felt more blessed.

epilogue

Seven years later

Mark set up a second card table in the living room. In a matter of minutes, almost the entire family would arrive to finish setting up for Kelly's surprise fiftieth birthday party. Mark hadn't been convinced it was the best of ideas with Zoey having just delivered their daughter four weeks ago, but everyone had outvoted him.

His five-year-old son, Tim, jerked on his shirt. "Dad, I put the napkins on the table like you said. What else can I do?"

Mark patted Zoey's father's namesake on the top of his carrot-colored head. "Go check on your brother."

"Okay."

"He was in my room the last I checked." Mark cringed at the thought of three-year-old Sam, his father's namesake, trying to play preschool games on the computer.

Mark walked into the kitchen, wending his way between Brittany, Sadie, and his mother until he finally reached Zoey. "What can I do to help now?"

She handed him their newest addition. "Take Maddy for me."

Mark walked into the living room and gently sat down in the recliner. He watched his sleeping infant. Their third child and first girl had been given his sister's name. Her full head of sandy-colored hair, just like Maddy's, felt like a small kiss from God.

Only three months after their wedding, his sister passed away. He'd never felt such sorrow. Not when his colleague

Kevin died. Not when his dad died. He and Maddy had been close, even as children, long before she became sick. But God saw him through the pain. He used Zoey to help. Now in His immeasurable goodness, God had given him a little sandy-haired girl. He lifted her tiny face to his lips and pressed a soft kiss on her cheek.

"When are you going to let Uncle Logan hold her?" Mark's tall, thin brother-in-law stood over him. "You know I need the practice."

Mark chuckled. "Okay." He stood and placed Maddy in Logan's arms.

"You look wonderful, honey." A seven-months-pregnant Brittany walked up beside Logan and caressed Maddy's leg. "You'll make a terrific daddy."

"Where's my granddaughter?" His mother, Sylvia, walked into the room. He'd been so worried about her when Maddy died. His father's death had triggered depression and panic attacks in his mother, and she did struggle again after Maddy's death. Until Zoey had her first grandchild. It was as if God used Tim to lift his mother out of despair and show her she still had purpose in life. Now she watched the children so that Zoey could continue doing the dietician job she loved. His mother kissed the top of Maddy's head. She winked at Logan. "Looks like she's in good hands. I'll go find the boys."

Zoey walked into the room. "Mark, do you know where my cell phone is? I can't find it, and Candy and Brad aren't here yet, and I need to tell them where to park so Mom doesn't see their car. . . ."

Mark wrapped his arms around Zoey and kissed her lips. "Calm down." She bit the inside of her mouth and squinted at him. "Remember, you promised I could kiss you anytime I wanted."

A smile bowed her lips. "I remember."

He patted his pocket. "I'll call your sister and her fiancé on my cell phone."

"Okay." She turned and disappeared back into the kitchen.

Fifteen-year-old Ellie walked up to him. The teen was beautiful with her long, flowing brown hair and deep brown eyes. Mark knew Cam had a hard time keeping the high school boys away. "Do you care if the twins and Micah and I set up a board game in the basement?"

Mark shook his head. "Don't mind at all. Just be ready to come back upstairs when Kelly gets here."

Mark watched as Micah, the lone boy, followed Ellie and the twins to the basement. Micah could have easily been his own son. He looked so much like Tim and Sam, who favored their mother. And Mark did have a soft spot for his wife's first biological child. But he was also happy for Cam to have a son. After adopting three girls—ages three, four, and five—from Romania, as well as already having Ellie, Cam needed at least one other guy in the house.

"Candy's here," Sadie yelled from the other room.

Mark cringed. He'd forgotten to call her when Ellie asked about going to the basement.

"Don't worry, Zoey"—Mark could hear Candy's voice from the other room—"we parked around the corner. We got a flat and Brad had to change it, and. . ."

Mark's phone vibrated in his front pocket. He pulled it out and read the name on the front. "Everyone be quiet," he hollered. "It's Harold."

Silence wrapped the packed house as Mark clicked his phone on. Harold's hushed voice sounded over the line. "I didn't have to trick her. She asked me to stop by your house so she can see the baby. We'll be there in ten minutes."

"Who are you talking to?" Mark grinned as he heard Kelly's

voice in the background.

"It's Mark." Harold's answer was muffled. "I'm telling him we're stopping by." He spoke back into the phone. "Ten minutes."

Mark clicked the phone off. "They'll be here in ten minutes."

The room flew into action as Cam called downstairs to get the kids. Mark's mother came out of one of the back bedrooms with the younger boys. Sadie and Cam, Candy and Brad, Brittany and Logan, and Kelly's parents all gathered together in the living area.

Zoey peeked out the front blinds. "I see them. Everyone ready?" She put her finger to her lips. "Quiet as a mouse until I open the door."

The doorbell rang, and Zoey opened the door. Choruses of "Surprise!" rang out through the room until Maddy squealed in protest.

Tears filled Kelly's eyes as she walked into the room and hugged each member of her family. Harold approached Mark and shook his hand. "We got her good."

Mark laughed as Harold made his way to Kelly, who was already holding and soothing Maddy. Mark watched the hustle and bustle of his family. Children romped everywhere. Adults talked and laughed. The noise was deafening. And he loved it.

When he'd met Zoey, his only concern was to lose enough weight that he wouldn't have to take blood pressure medicine, that he would be healthy. Eight years had passed since he met his wife, and he'd kept the weight off and still didn't need the medication.

But he'd gained more than he'd ever lost. He gained more extended family than he ever would have dreamed. He gained a wife and three beautiful children.

He sucked in a long breath. *God, when I walked into that*

gym, all I cared about was losing, but You had other plans.
I did lose, but I also gained.

I gained love.

A Letter To Our Readers

Dear Reader:

In order that we might better contribute to your reading enjoyment, we would appreciate your taking a few minutes to respond to the following questions. We welcome your comments and read each form and letter we receive. When completed, please return to the following:

Fiction Editor
Heartsong Presents
PO Box 719
Uhrichsville, Ohio 44683

1. Did you enjoy reading *Gaining Love* by Jennifer Johnson?
   ❏ Very much! I would like to see more books by this author!
   ❏ Moderately. I would have enjoyed it more if

   _____

   _____

   _____

2. Are you a member of **Heartsong Presents**? ❏ Yes ❏ No
   If no, where did you purchase this book? _____

   _____

3. How would you rate, on a scale from 1 (poor) to 5 (superior), the cover design? _____

4. On a scale from 1 (poor) to 10 (superior), please rate the following elements.

   ____ Heroine   ____ Plot
   ____ Hero   ____ Inspirational theme
   ____ Setting   ____ Secondary characters

5. These characters were special because? _____

_____

_____

6. How has this book inspired your life? _____

_____

_____

7. What settings would you like to see covered in future
   Heartsong Presents books? _____

_____

_____

8. What are some inspirational themes you would like to see
   treated in future books? _____

_____

_____

9. Would you be interested in reading other **Heartsong
   Presents** titles? ❏ Yes ❏ No

10. Please check your age range:
    ❏ Under 18   ❏ 18-24
    ❏ 25-34   ❏ 35-45
    ❏ 46-55   ❏ Over 55

Name _____

Occupation _____

Address _____

City, State, Zip_____

E-mail _____

LOVE IS MONUMENTAL

National Park Ranger Vickie Harris loves her job assignment at the Washington Monument in her nation's capital. But while her life in the District of Columbia is exciting and fun, the shy and withdrawn Vickie has resigned herself to the likelihood of being single forever.

Contemporary, paperback, 320 pages, 5⅜" x 8"

—————————————————————

Please send me ____ copies of *Love is Monumental*. I am enclosing $12.99 for each.
(Please add $4.00 to cover postage and handling per order. OH add 7% tax.
If outside the U.S. please call 740-922-7280 for shipping charges.)

Name _____

Address _____

City, State, Zip _____

To place a credit card order, call 1-740-922-7280.
Send to: Heartsong Presents Readers' Service, PO Box 721, Uhrichsville, OH 44683

Heartsong

Any 12 Heartsong Presents titles for only $27.00*

CONTEMPORARY ROMANCE IS CHEAPER BY THE DOZEN!

Buy any assortment of twelve *Heartsong Presents* titles and save 25% off the already discounted price of $2.97 each!

*plus $4.00 shipping and handling per order and sales tax where applicable.
If outside the U.S. please call 740-922-7280 for shipping charges.

HEARTSONG PRESENTS TITLES AVAILABLE NOW:

___HP645 *The Hunt for Home*, G. Aiken
___HP649 *4th of July*, J. Livingston
___HP650 *Romanian Rhapsody*, D. Franklin
___HP653 *Lakeside*, M. Davis
___HP654 *Alaska Summer*, M. H. Flinkman
___HP657 *Love Worth Finding*, C. M. Hake
___HP658 *Love Worth Keeping*, J. Livingston
___HP661 *Lambert's Code*, R. Hauck
___HP665 *Bah Humbug, Mrs. Scrooge*, J. Livingston
___HP666 *Sweet Charity*, J. Thompson
___HP669 *The Island*, M. Davis
___HP670 *Miss Menace*, N. Lavo
___HP673 *Flash Flood*, D. Mills
___HP677 *Banking on Love*, J. Thompson
___HP678 *Lambert's Peace*, R. Hauck
___HP681 *The Wish*, L. Bliss
___HP682 *The Grand Hotel*, M. Davis
___HP685 *Thunder Bay*, B. Loughner
___HP686 *Always a Bridesmaid*, A. Boeshaar
___HP689 *Unforgettable*, J. L. Barton
___HP690 *Heritage*, M. Davis
___HP693 *Dear John*, K. V. Sawyer
___HP694 *Riches of the Heart*, T. Davis
___HP697 *Dear Granny*, P. Griffin
___HP698 *With a Mother's Heart*, J. Livingston
___HP701 *Cry of My Heart*, L. Ford
___HP702 *Never Say Never*, L. N. Dooley
___HP705 *Listening to Her Heart*, J. Livingston
___HP706 *The Dwelling Place*, K. Miller
___HP709 *That Wilder Boy*, K. V. Sawyer
___HP710 *To Love Again*, J. L. Barton
___HP713 *Secondhand Heart*, J. Livingston
___HP714 *Anna's Journey*, N. Toback
___HP717 *Merely Players*, K. Kovach
___HP718 *In His Will*, C. Hake
___HP721 *Through His Grace*, K. Hake
___HP722 *Christmas Mommy*, T. Fowler

___HP725 *By His Hand*, J. Johnson
___HP726 *Promising Angela*, K. V. Sawyer
___HP729 *Bay Hideaway*, B. Loughner
___HP730 *With Open Arms*, J. L. Barton
___HP733 *Safe in His Arms*, T. Davis
___HP734 *Larkspur Dreams*, A. Higman and J. A. Thompson
___HP737 *Darcy's Inheritance*, L. Ford
___HP738 *Picket Fence Pursuit*, J. Johnson
___HP741 *The Heart of the Matter*, K. Dykes
___HP742 *Prescription for Love*, A. Boeshaar
___HP745 *Family Reunion*, J. L. Barton
___HP746 *By Love Acquitted*, Y. Lehman
___HP749 *Love by the Yard*, G. Sattler
___HP750 *Except for Grace*, T. Fowler
___HP753 *Long Trail to Love*, P. Griffin
___HP754 *Red Like Crimson*, J. Thompson
___HP757 *Everlasting Love*, L. Ford
___HP758 *Wedded Bliss*, K. Y'Barbo
___HP761 *Double Blessing*, D. Mayne
___HP762 *Photo Op*, L. A. Coleman
___HP765 *Sweet Sugared Love*, P. Griffin
___HP766 *Pursuing the Goal*, J. Johnson
___HP769 *Who Am I?*, L. N. Dooley
___HP770 *And Baby Makes Five*, G. G. Martin
___HP773 *A Matter of Trust*, L. Harris
___HP774 *The Groom Wore Spurs*, J. Livingston
___HP777 *Seasons of Love*, E. Goddard
___HP778 *The Love Song*, J. Thompson
___HP781 *Always Yesterday*, J. Odell
___HP782 *Trespassed Hearts*, L. A. Coleman
___HP785 *If the Dress Fits*, D. Mayne
___HP786 *White as Snow*, J. Thompson
___HP789 *The Bride Wore Coveralls*, D. Ullrick
___HP790 *Garlic and Roses*, G. Martin
___HP793 *Coming Home*, T. Fowler
___HP794 *John's Quest*, C. Dowdy
___HP797 *Building Dreams*, K. Y'Barbo

(If ordering from this page, please remember to include it with the order form.)

Presents

HEARTSONG
PRESENTS

If you love Christian romance...

$10.99

You'll love Heartsong Presents' inspiring and faith-filled romances by today's very best Christian authors. . .Wanda E. Brunstetter, Mary Connealy, Susan Page Davis, Cathy Marie Hake, and Joyce Livingston, to mention a few!

When you join Heartsong Presents, you'll enjoy four brand-new, mass-market, 176-page books—two contemporary and two historical—that will build you up in your faith when you discover God's role in every relationship you read about!

Imagine. . .four new romances every four weeks—with men and women like you who long to meet the one God has chosen as the love of their lives...all for the low price of $10.99 postpaid.

Mass Market 176 Pages

To join, simply visit www.heartsong presents.com or complete the coupon below and mail it to the address provided.

- -

YES! Sign me up for Heartsong!

NEW MEMBERSHIPS WILL BE SHIPPED IMMEDIATELY!
Send no money now. We'll bill you only $10.99 postpaid with your first shipment of four books. Or for faster action, call 1-740-922-7280.

NAME_____

ADDRESS_____

CITY_____ STATE _____ ZIP _____

MAIL TO: HEARTSONG PRESENTS, P.O. Box 721, Uhrichsville, Ohio 44683
or sign up at WWW.HEARTSONGPRESENTS.COM